SABOTAGE

PIET PRINS

The Shadow Series 5

INHERITANCE PUBLICATIONS
NEERLANDIA, ALBERTA, CANADA

Canadian Cataloguing in Publication Data

Prins, Piet, 1909-1984
  Sabotage
  (Shadow series ; 5)
  Translation of: *Van strijd en overwinning.*

  ISBN 0-921100-08-6

  1. Wold War, 1939-1945 - Underground movements -
Netherlands - Juvenile fiction. 2. Netherlands - History - German
occupation, 1940-1945 - Juvenile fiction. I. Title. II. Series: Prins,
Piet, 1909- Shadow series ; 5
PT5866.P7V3613 1989   j839.3'13'64   C89-091150-9

First published in Dutch as *Holland onder het hakenkruis, IV Van
Strijd en Overwinning,* c. Jacob Dijkstra's Uitgeverij N.V.,
Groningen.

Translated by James C. van Oosterom.
Cover painting by Cornelia Van Dasselaar
Illustrations by Jaap Kramer

ISBN 0-921100-08-6

Printed in Canada by
Premier Printing Ltd. Winnipeg, MB

TITLES IN THE SHADOW SERIES

Table of Contents

CHAPTER ONE

THE ARDENNES COUNTEROFFENSIVE

In the dark month of December 1944, the sun seemed to have given up. Cold rain poured down between snow flurries. Heavy fighting continued on nearly all fronts, but the Allied armies seemed to make little progress. Troops were shivering and freezing in their trenches. The bad weather caused extra illness. Everybody hoped that spring would bring the end of the war. Just a few more months . . .

But Hitler had different ideas. He wasn't about to admit defeat. In fact, he was busy working out a plan that might still turn the tide in his favour again.

The German fuhrer knew that Marshal Montgomery had dug his British troops into the southern provinces of the Netherlands. Farther south, in the provinces of Alsace-Lorraine, French troops and the strong American army under General Patton waited. Between, in the eastern parts of Belgium and Luxembourg, in the hilly, wooded, and snow-covered region known as the Ardennes, the Allied front was·dangerously thin. And that front was stretched out over a distance of 130 kilometres. German intelligence had learned about this weak area.

Secretly, in the dark of night, Hitler assembled a massive army of a quarter of a million soldiers directly opposite the weak sector of the Allied front. This army was manned and equipped with the best Germany had available: fanatical S.S. divisions and armed divisions numbering thousands of modern tanks. Although the German Luftwaffe had already lost air superiority, every available unit was sent to the Ardennes to provide air cover for the coming assault.

Even though these German troops were assembled in absolute secrecy, the Allies suspected something. But they didn't do anything about it, assuming that Germany was on its last legs. In the event Hitler

tried something in the Ardennes, Montgomery and Patton should be able to close in for defense from north and south.

At Allied headquarters nobody had any idea about the strength and determination of the desperate Germans. On December 15, the Germans were ready to move. Of the seventy divisions stationed along the western front, they had assembled twenty-nine—all of them crack troops—for a lightning strike through the Ardennes. The panzer divisions would blitz through the four American divisions stationed in the Ardennes and continue on to Liege, Brussels, and Antwerp, where the harbour was being used by Allies to supply their armies at the front.

If the Germans succeeded, Montgomery's troops, now lodged in Zeeland, Noord Brabant, and Limburg, would be cut off from their supplies and from the American armies to the south. It would mean a tremendous military and moral victory for Hitler. Even if it didn't bring about the total collapse of the Allies, it would buy time. Time would give Germany the opportunity to perfect its new weapon systems: a new U-boat fleet and new missiles. Once these weapons were in operation, Hitler was sure he could win the war.

Within the ranks of the formidable German force was one panzer brigade with a very special assignment. They all wore American uniforms and were equipped with American weapons and vehicles. They all spoke fluent English with an American accent because they were men who had lived in the United States for a while. The weapons, uniforms, and vehicles had been captured at other fronts and assembled here.

These men knew their task; the minute the advance German guard had blitzed through the American lines, they were to spread out and mingle among the American troops in order to sow confusion, occupy strategic positions, and countermand genuine American army orders. It was Hitler himself who had come up with the idea, and he had high hopes for it.

Saturday, December 16, 5:30 A.M.: Only the snow on the fields softened the darkness. But not a single German soldier was asleep. Thousands of German soldiers waited tensely beside their artillery pieces, anxious for the order to open fire.

At 5:30 sharp, the command came: "Fire!" Instantly hundreds of artillery pieces and howitzers rained down death and destruction on the American lines in the Ardennes.

Then, with their job well done, the cannons fell silent and the tanks and armoured vehicles swung into action. Like a landslide of steel they rolled into the Ardennes right over American positions. An umbrella of Luftwaffe planes supported the action on the ground and bombed American positions to the rear.

There was no way the Americans could hold their positions. Many were mowed down where they stood. Some tried desperately to retreat to more secure positions. Some of them fought back stubbornly until they were killed or ran out of ammunition.

The German forces, superior in both strength and numbers, poured through.

General Eisenhower, headquartered in Paris, was shaken when he heard of the assault. He moved immediately to counter the thrust. The English armies to the north and the American armies to the south were ordered to send reinforcements to close the gap. But that could only happen after careful organization. For the time being, the few American troops in the Ardennes were left to fend for themselves.

The first three days of the assault were like a nightmare. There was confusion everywhere. The brigade of Germans impersonating Americans created havoc and uncertainty just as planned. Trust vanished. Even high-ranking American officers trying to reestablish contact with their units were picked up by the military police and examined because they could very well have been Germans in disguise.

Some self-confidence returned to the German army. Germany would now show that tenderfoot army from backwoods America how to fight a war! Germany had been destined all along to win this war, and that's exactly what was going to happen! On to Antwerp!

But the Germans were sadly mistaken in their new hope that the Americans were bumbling cowards. After the initial shock, the Americans quickly recovered. They no longer fled in disarray but found more secure positions and dug in stubbornly.

Bitter fighting broke out on all the snow-covered hills and in the thick forests of the Ardennes. Hopelessly outnumbered, the Americans knew they couldn't last long. But when they were forced to withdraw, they did so in orderly fashion and quickly established themselves in new strategic positions.

German arrogance gave way to surprise and uncertainty. The thrust to Antwerp wasn't going as smoothly as expected. Had they underestimated the Americans?

Indeed, the Americans could still fight. The most telling example was their heroic defense of the city of Bastogne. Bastogne was right in the middle of the Ardennes, at the junction of seven major roads. If the Germans were to succeed in their quick drive to the sea, they would have to take and hold Bastogne.

The German high command didn't think that Bastogne would be much of a problem. The American troops were surrounded on all sides with their supply lines cut. German panzer divisions were continuing on to the west. But Bastogne was taking too long.

The city was defended by American troops that had been fighting desperately for three days and had finally withdrawn to this point. The Germans figured that since the Americans couldn't possibly get help, they would probably surrender.

A German officer was sent to Bastogne with an ultimatum demanding the American garrison's immediate, unconditional surrender. If the garrison refused, it would be totally annihilated! The American commander calmly read the terms of the surrender, took out a piece of paper, and scribbled down his reply. His official reply was one word--"Nuts."

When the Germans realized what that one word meant, they were enraged and began their attack.

Along a perimeter about twenty kilometres outside the city of Bastogne, the Americans dug in, determined not to give an inch.

The Germans attacked relentlessly for almost four days. A panzer division and a grenadier division armed with mortars tried to destroy American resistance. But the thin perimeter withstood the attack, despite the heavy losses.

On Christmas Eve the Germans threw everything they had at the defenders. Bombs, grenades, artillery, and howitzer shells rained down on Bastogne. Heavy tanks, firing incessantly, lumbered across the battle-torn landscape to try to break American resistance. Behind them came the German infantry. Two battalions of Wehrmacht soldiers penetrated American lines, but the tough defenders threw them back in hand-to-hand combat. Eighteen German tanks that had managed to break through the lines were wiped out before they reached the city. American troops inside mopped up anything that came through the lines. Bastogne could not be taken on Christmas Eve.

On both Christmas and the following day, the Germans tried harder. The Americans already had five hundred dead and twenty-five wounded, but every able-bodied man, however exhausted, fought on grimly.

On December 26, at about 3:00 in the afternoon, the advance guard of an American armoured division reached the hills to the south of the city. Before the night fell, Bastogne had been rescued!

The man in charge of the relief force was General Patton, whose men had fought and marched for seven days to get to Bastogne in time. In the process they had lost a thousand men and two-thirds of their inventory, but they had succeeded.

Other American and English divisions were rushing from the north and south to halt the German push westward and to protect the Meuse River.

During the week before Christmas, the weather had been so bad that not a single airplane had left the ground. But on December 23, the cloud cover suddenly broke, and for a week after that there was nothing but sunshine. That was unusual for the end of December, and for the Allies it was a great relief. Now they could get their fighters and bombers airborne and pound the German advance from above.

The German advance westward wasn't halted, but it was slowed down. Again the Germans tried to capture Bastogne; they really had no choice. As long as this crucial junction remained in Allied hands, the Germans had only one good paved road along which to send supplies and reinforcements. They threw ten more divisions into the battle of Bastogne. The conflict seesawed back and forth, but after all they had suffered already, the Americans were determined not to vacate the city.

Aerial combat was bitter; two thousand American bombers, supported by eight hundred fighters, flew into the battle of the Ardennes. Within days, the Allies had air superiority.

The further the Germans moved west, the harder their job was. As a result, they had to narrow their assault more and more. Finally their attacking line was little more than a wedge pointing deep into enemy-held territory toward the Meuse River. Despite a final concentrated effort to capture the bridges, the German armies failed to take the Meuse.

With the sun came bitter-cold temperatures. There was much snow on the ground. All the soldiers suffered from the cold, but this was especially true for the Germans. They were not very warmly dressed and were poorly fed. Their morale slumped. Their arrogance and self-confidence vanished as they sensed they had lost one of the most critical battles of the war.

As soon as the German attack ground to a halt, it was time for an Allied counteroffensive. The British attacked from the north, the Americans from the south.

Though demoralized, Hitler's armies weren't finished yet. They fought heroically for every kilometre, but their hopes for victory were gone, and gradually they lost ground. At the end of January, the front was exactly where it had been a month and a half before. Hitler's desperate effort had failed.

The Germans had lost 120,000 men, sixteen hundred aircraft, six hundred tanks, and six thousand vehicles. Despite these enormous losses, the German high command managed to evacuate the larger part of its gigantic army.

The Allies losses were heavy but not incapacitating. The Allies were still well supplied and had the upper hand.

With the failure of his Ardennes offensive, Hitler had lost his last chance. And yet he ordered his men to fight on until the bitter end.

CHAPTER TWO

A PLAN OF ACTION

Winter had definitely settled in; a weak, watery sun hung low in a pearl-grey sky. On all the rooftops around the warehouse, lay several centimetres of snow.

Blankers was sitting near his window high up in his attic bedroom. Gerritsen was somewhere downstairs in the warehouse and his wife was in the kitchen doing the dishes. She had declined Blankers' offer of help. She thought he'd be better off keeping watch at the window because there was every chance that Willem or some of the other men of the Resistance would come by today. In that case, the quicker they were let in the better.

Blankers was depressed. Christmas had come and gone, and within a few days, it would be New Year's Day. He missed his wife and children much more than usual. It had even occurred to him that he should try to see them. After all, now that he had a mustache and spectacles, he looked like somebody else altogether.

But he had resisted that urge immediately. He had done that once before, with disastrous consequences. No, he'd never try it again!

What was he complaining about anyway? He scolded himself. He couldn't possibly have found a better place. Oom Koos and Tante Miep took excellent care of him, although with each passing day the rations were getting slimmer. And yet . . .

There was something that bothered him. For the first time in months, it was the Germans who were doing the attacking. Everybody had thought that the war was practically over, and then the Germans had broken through Allied defenses in the Ardennes. The "reorganized" (Nazi) Dutch radio had described the details of the German victory enthusiastically. The result was that the morale of most Dutch people had plummeted just like the temperature outside!

14

The worst seemed to be over; Radio Orange announced that the Americans had successfully defended the city of Bastogne. But the Germans were still advancing westward.

It was too much for poor Blankers. Would there never be an end to German tyranny? How long would people have to suffer and bleed under the yoke of this oppressor?

If only he could do something for the war effort. What was the good of just sitting here and waiting? True, he had a role to play in Resistance work, but it seemed so insignificant.

Blankers' mind was wandering through discouraging thoughts when a familiar signal sounded. Sure enough, there was Willem, huddled in a grey overcoat, his hat pulled down over his eyes.

Blankers quickly tripped the latch opening the door to the courtyard. Willem came in, closing the door behind him. Then he walked up to the warehouse.

Several minutes passed before he came into the attic bedroom, accompanied by Oom Koos. He looked cheerful but realized immediately that Blankers was not in the best of moods.

"What's the matter, man? You look depressed."

"Oh, no," Blankers hedged, ashamed that it was so obvious. "It's only that . . . well, doing nothing is getting the better of me, and this war is taking such a long time."

"That's for sure, but we'll do everything we can do to shorten it. Besides, there's something I want you to do! We'll leave tonight."

He pulled a chair up to the stove's heat and rubbed his hands. Blankers and Gerritsen joined him. Apparently Willem had something important to discuss.

"The Germans are up to something," he said. "Intelligence has it that they're concentrating troops in our country—at least three divisions. They're probably planning to cross the Meuse and get to Antwerp to meet their colleagues from the Ardennes. That means that the Allied troops in our southern provinces will be caught in a panzer movement. We're going to have to delay the movement as much as possible by blowing up the railroads. We've got the explosives for it."

That was significant! Now Blankers was getting excited. He knew that the Germans had managed, despite the general rail strike, to open some of the more important rail lines for military traffic. Those lines were now manned by Germans and used exclusively for the German war effort. Blowing up the railways and causing German train derailments could help neutralize their power.

Willem spelled out the details. That night they had to blow up at least two railways. He had already picked out the best places. If they were successful, any German troop movement would be delayed for several days.

The whole squad would be activated. The leader would visit each of the members individually and pass on instructions. Later that afternoon Cor would come by with a car to pick up Blankers, now called Gerard de Wit. They would have to load up the explosives. Then they would pick up the other men.

Their plan outlined, they went down into the cellar to fetch the supplies. Willem, who knew most about this sort of thing, decided what they needed. Judging from the amount of explosives he took, it was clear that he didn't want to do a half-job.

"It looks like you're going to blow up the whole Dutch railway system tonight," observed Oom Koos.

"If only that were possible! In any case, I'd rather take too much than too little." They also decided to take along some derailers, massive triangular pieces of metal to be attached to the rails to make the locomotive tip.

"Well, I guess that'll be enough. Load this stuff up in some crates and cover it with a layer of potatoes. We'll bring back what we don't need, including potatoes. And Gerard, don't forget to bring your revolver. Cor will be here with the van at about three o'clock. Make sure you're ready. Well, see you later, and say hello to Tante Miep!"

When Willem left, Blankers began to wrap the dangerous material in paper and stuff it into large wooden crates. Then he fetched the potatoes to cover it all up. Blankers realized that this could be dangerous. Well, this is what he had wished for; he had wanted action. But now he felt a bit uneasy about it. He was really no adventurer. He didn't like to take chances, but he knew this had to be done. He was a soldier now, just like any young American fighting in the Ardennes staring death in the face for the benefit of mankind.

At a quarter to three, Cor showed up. He drove the van into the warehouse, and the two men loaded up the sabotage materials. Blankers stuck his revolver into his pocket and went to the back of the van. Cor slid behind the steering wheel and drove off.

They stopped at various places in the city to pick up the other members of the Resistance, including Willem, who sat up front with Cor. The others joined Blankers in the back.

Once they had picked up the last man, Cor stepped on the gas. Soon they had left the suburbs behind. By looking through the holes in the sides of the van, the men could see glimpses of the outside world, but it was already close to four o'clock and dark was falling.

The men didn't say much; each was engrossed in his own thoughts, tense with anxiety about how this would end. They had no idea where they were going. The only ones who knew were Willem and Cor.

Out on the big highway, they soon came to a viaduct. Here Cor turned off and drove for about three hundred metres until they came to an inn at the side of a road that had been the main traffic artery before the new highway was built.

They stopped in front of the inn. Willem got out and went into the lounge. A couple of minutes later, he came back and opened the van's rear doors.

"Come on out, guys. The coast is clear."

Cor drove the van into a large shed beside the inn and then joined the others in the lounge. Beside the six of them, there was no one there but the innkeeper's wife. She greeted the men, showed them to a large table, and brought them something warm to drink.

Willem told his men that they would stay here until their guide showed up.

Waiting is always unnerving, especially at a time like this. They amused themselves by smoking cigarettes and talking to each other in undertones. Soon the innkeeper's wife brought the men a large pot of pea soup and some bowls and spoons. It was tasty and hot, and the men had no trouble putting it all away.

Around seven o'clock a boy of about fifteen came into the lounge. He went straight to the bar and exchanged a few words with the innkeeper's wife. Together they came over to the table.

"This is Peter, your guide," explained the woman. All the men looked surprised. Willem knitted his eyebrows and said brusquely, "This is not child's play, you know! Don't you have a better guide?" The boy blushed but didn't flinch. He had an indignant look on his face. The innkeeper's wife put her hand on his shoulder and explained, "You don't know Peter. This isn't the first time he's risked his neck. You can't find a better guide, except maybe his dad. Well, his dad worked for the railroad and is not around because he's in hiding. Peter knows these parts better that anybody else. In fact, when he was only knee high, he went with his dad everywhere."

While she was explaining, Willem watched the boy intently. Apparently he was satisfied, because by the time the woman had finished her explanation, he held out his hand. "I'm glad you're with us. You'll have to excuse my reaction. That was stupid of me. There are a lot of boys like you who are worth more than most men."

Peter only smiled and shook Willem's hand. He looked like a quiet person with deep thoughts and spirit. The sparkle in his eyes seemed to confirm his depth. For just a second Blankers was reminded of his own brave son who was only a couple of years younger than this boy. Peter glanced up at the clock behind the bar and said, "It's time to go. We'll need about fifteen minutes to get there." Willem, Cor, and Blankers fetched the explosives from the van, and each of the men was given something to carry. Then they stealthily slipped out into the darkness.

CHAPTER THREE

THE RAILWAY BRIDGE DYNAMITED

By now it was completely dark and overcast; there was not a single star to guide them. Peter was up front, leading them along the road that went under the viaduct and eventually came to a wide canal. Just for a moment he looked up and down the bank. The men couldn't see a thing, but in no time at all Peter had located a flat-bottomed scow.

It was a clumsy rectangular craft but ideal for their purpose. Gingerly they lowered themselves into the boat, but Meijer wasn't quite careful enough. He would have ended up in the water had it not been for Cor, who grabbed him by the arm.

The boy released the rope and grabbed one of the punting poles while Blankers took the other. They pushed off toward the middle of the stream and then drifted down with the current.

Everyone was silent, and the two sailors punted as noiselessly as they could. Blankers had had lots of practice punting back in the marsh.

After about five minutes, they maneuvered the craft to the other side of the canal. The rope was slung and pulled tight around an elderberry bush. The men clambered up the side of the dike.

They followed the dike for about a hundred metres before the boy suddenly halted. By now they had all become used to the darkness, and they could vaguely see the silhouette of a house dead ahead.

"That's our house," Peter whispered. "They kicked us out when Dad went on strike. It was taken over by the Germans who operate the tracks and the switches. There's always a guard outside the house and another one on the other side of the bridge. If we stay on this dike, we'll be able to slip in behind him and get to the bridge, but we'll have to be very careful."

Two of the men wore rubber-soled shoes, and the others sat down to wrap pieces of an old blanket around their shoes to muffle sound.

Willem then gave them his final instructions. "Peter, you and Heins keep watch on this side of the bridge. The rest of you come with me to the middle of the bridge. Once we get there, Cor, Gerard, and I will tie down the explosives. Meijer and Dijkmans, you two continue on to the other side of the bridge to cover us. If anything happens, you'll have to take care of each other; stay alert, but don't get trigger happy."

The railroad lay straight ahead of them; about fifty metres off to the left was Peter's former house. They could just hear the sound of the German guard walking back and forth.

Heins and Peter took up their positions here while the others sneaked out onto the bridge. Twenty metres out onto the bridge Blankers' foot dislodged a small pebble that rolled down the side of the bank.

They all lay flat on their stomachs for about a minute. Nothing happened. Then Willem whispered a warning: "Watch it, Gerard. Pick up your feet."

Silently, Blankers rebuked himself. It was all because of those clumsy blankets wrapped around his feet. And then this darkness was thick as pea soup. It was precisely the darkness they needed; without it, they wouldn't have a chance.

On they went again. This time Blankers walked like a cat picking its way through a wet grassy field. Finally, they were in the middle of the bridge. Dijkmans and Meijer put down the explosives they had been carrying and walked on to the far end of the bridge.

Willem knelt down beside the tracks, feeling along the iron rail until he found a suitable spot for a time bomb.

"Two sticks," he whispered. Blankers knew what he wanted. Plastic dynamite, very convenient stuff—you could knead it and shape it like a lump of dough. It seemed completely harmless. Even if you held a flame to it, it wouldn't explode. To make it explode you needed a special detonator, and then the explosive reaction was tremendous. Willem secured the sticks; into them he inserted a plug of a slightly more sensitive explosive. Then he applied the detonator cap. Just before attaching the pencil, Willem had to check it to see if it was the right one. It had to be one with a white pin, indicating it would go off in two hours.

Willem worked feverishly for a couple of minutes. The sooner they got out of there the better, but he knew they couldn't rush this. The slightest mistake could mean immediate disaster or the failure of the explosive to detonate at all.

Finally he breathed deeply and straightened up. The bomb was set! Blankers thought they'd go back now, but he was wrong. Willem informed him that he wanted to fix a much heavier charge to the bottom of the railway bridge.

That was a lot trickier. Lying on his stomach, Blankers passed all the materials to Cor, who hung from the side of the rail and in turn passed everything to Willem. Willem was hanging upside down with his legs wrapped around the rails so that he could use both hands to fix the charge. He was sweating now; it was even more important to position this charge correctly.

Blankers stood in awe of his two associates. They were hanging high above the water, and if they fell—well, even if they survived that, the splash would certainly bring a whole platoon of German soldiers down on their backs.

What a relief when Cor and Willem scrambled back up! Now they could start back.

While Cor and Willem gathered up the remaining supplies, Blankers inched his way to Meijer and Dijkmans to tell them it was over and that they were going back. Then the five of them made their way back to where Heins and Peter were waiting.

Willem's only comment to the other men was, "Okay, it's all set! It's going off in two hours. Seen anything special?"

"No, nothing. That sentry's still there, but he never noticed a thing."

They made their way down the dike to where they had moored the scow. With each step they were getting farther and farther from danger.

Blankers felt rather proud of himself. He had stayed cool throughout the whole caper. But then, he admitted, his part hadn't been the most dangerous. He'd been through nothing like Cor and Willem.

The scow was still there, and they quickly descended and punted away.

Ten minutes later they were back at the inn to take a second load of explosives from the van. This time they punted off in the other direction. Just as they pushed off, they heard the sound of truck engines above them. A large military column thundered across the viaduct.

The seven men in the scow ducked down to avoid being seen. Nobody moved a muscle.

Anybody who looked down from the viaduct might be able to see the scow in the water's reflection, despite the darkness. And the Germans would undoubtedly investigate a scow floating in a canal.

One after another the trucks roared past. It was only a matter of a few minutes, but to the men in the boat it seemed like hours.

With the last truck gone, the men still kept from moving just to make sure that no one was coming back to investigate. Only when they were absolutely sure did they pick up the punting poles and move off again. Even now, though the immediate danger had passed, nobody said a word.

All around them a mysterious darkness enshrouded the landscape. The only sign of life was the gentle splashing of the punting poles in the water.

They had a lot farther to go this time. It was cold so close to the water in the middle of the winter. The men took turns punting, and each one was happy when it was his turn because the movement restored his circulation.

At last Peter signalled them to shore. They moored the boat next to a dilapidated windmill and continued on foot across the meadow. Against the white background of snow, they knew they could be spotted. But they trusted that no German or Dutch civilian police would be out in this deserted landscape at night.

They were even more worried about the footprints they were leaving in the snow. That would work against them if they were followed. That's actually why they had come most of the way by boat; on the water they didn't leave any telltale signs.

But no need to worry about that. Tomorrow at about this time they'd be safe and sound in the city. It would take an expert tracker to follow their trail all the way back there.

After plodding across the field, they came to a wide ditch. Behind it was their destination, the rail dike. The ice on the ditch would be thin, so Peter led them along the side of it until they came to a dam. Once across it, Willem took charge, whispering instructions to each of the men.

There was a double line here which had been used only sparingly since the railway strike, but there were indications that the Germans had been running supply and troop transports along here only recently.

Blowing up the rails wouldn't help much; the Germans would have that repaired in one day. A bridge was something else because it wasn't simply a matter of replacing the track; workers had to replace the trestles, too. But on the dike, the best thing would be to cause a derailment. That would cause a lot more damage, keeping the dike out of commission for several days at least.

At first Willem had planned to loosen a section of the rails in order to cause a derailment, but it was both too dark and too cold to get that done in time. So he chose to use a triangular derailer. Chances were reasonably good that the engineer wouldn't spot the device in time.

The derailer on the left rail of the track would cause the pilot wheels to veer off to the left; the one on the right was angled upward slightly and would lift the right pilot wheels up into the air. That way the engine would flip over to the left and block the other track as well.

Fastening the derailers down took less time than they had thought.

"What'll we do now?" Cor asked.

"I was just wondering about that." For the first time there was a trace of hesitancy in Willem's voice. Then he continued, "Up until now everything's gone just fine. Much quicker than I thought. We could pull one more caper, but we might be trying too much."

"What is it?" Cor asked again.

"Well, about ten minutes from here, this track joins the main line. Just beyond that, there's a yard. There are always lots of cars and engines there that are used by the Wehrmacht. I wouldn't mind slipping a couple of time bombs in there . . ."

The others thought it was an excellent idea and wanted to pursue it right away, but Willem cautioned them.

"Just a second. It's not as easy as all that. I'm sure that the yard is being patrolled night and day. If we just charge in there without a plan, it'll be a disaster. Peter, do you know the area?"

He did and assured the men that there were always extra patrols these days--sentries to watch the accesses, soldiers in the watch towers, and probably even special detachments to patrol the fields.

"Do you think you could take us to the cars without being seen?" Willem asked.

Peter didn't reply right away. He was thinking. Finally he said, "I know how you can get in; but once you're in the yard, you're on your own, and anything can happen."

"Well, what do you think, guys? Should we risk it or not?"

They discussed it briefly; most of them were inclined to do it. Had the successes so far made them a bit overconfident? Although Willem was always prepared to take some risks, he remained doubtful but finally submitted to his comrades' wishes.

Again Peter took the lead. They walked on until they came to the main line. Then they turned left, leaving the railway behind. The terrain became more wooded. They carefully made their way among the shrubs and trees, coming ever closer to their goal. The going was slow because they had to move silently. Snapping a single branch might be enough to alarm the German sentries.

All at once Peter stopped, listening attentively for a few seconds. He turned to Willem and whispered, "Wait here. I'm going to see if we can get in."

He slipped off and was soon swallowed up by the darkness.

CHAPTER FOUR

A PARTISAN PAYS THE PRICE

The men stayed huddled in the bushes. Blankers felt like the marrow of his bones was freezing. Then he had to fight back a sneeze.

The minutes passed until finally Peter showed up again. He whispered, "Come on. But watch out for the sentries!"

They crawled across the rugged snowy terrain on all fours, and the damp cold that soaked their clothes made them feel even colder than before. But to be back in action again helped them forget their discomfort.

Suddenly they came to a high chain-link fence. Against the fence, bushes and shrubs provided excellent cover.

Blankers stopped right beside Peter. His teeth were chattering as he whispered, "What now?"

"We wait until the sentry goes by," replied the boy.

That must have taken five minutes, and all the while the men lay on the frozen ground. Finally they heard footsteps approaching. That had to be the sentry covering the inside of the fence.

He passed by less than two metres away. If one of them had moved or made even the slightest sound, the sentry would have spotted them. They had the awful feeling that he must have seen them anyway, but that was just their imagination. The darkness and the shrubs gave them ample protection.

They waited with bated breath until the German's footsteps faded away.

Peter inched forward to a piece of wire fence that he had yanked loose from a post. He lifted the fence high enough for a man to crawl under it.

One after the other they slipped through the opening. Peter was the last to go through but then immediately took the lead again.

Silently they hurried across the compound, past stacks of railway ties and rows of switches to where a freight train was standing. This was the train they wanted to blow up.

Having reached their target without difficulty, they put the explosives down on the ground. Willem leaned forward to crawl under the train.

"Halt! Hande hoch!"[1] a loud German voice cut through the darkness of the winter night. Two spotlights were suddenly switched on, one of them focusing directly on the startled group of men.

---

[1] Stop! Put up your hands!

Confused, some of them put up their hands, knowing full well that the Germans would open fire unless they were obeyed. But Willem had already disappeared under the car. He immediately drew his revolver and fired two shots. From behind one of the spotlights came an agonized scream. The lamp clattered to the ground and went out.

Then Cor went into action. As he pulled the trigger of his submachine gun, the Germans also opened fire.

A bullet whistled past Blankers' head. The men scattered in all directions as the Germans kept firing indiscriminately. Cor's left arm had been hit, but his legs were all right. But Meijer fell down on the gravel, fatally wounded.

The remainder ran for their lives, trying desperately to avoid the spotlights. Six or eight soldiers were in hot pursuit, and more came running up from other directions.

They had to get back to the hole in the fence! That one thought was on Blankers' mind. He jumped across the tracks, stumbled, scrambled back up, and wildly ran on.

There was the gate, but he didn't want to go there. Where was the hole? Where was the hole? He knew that the top of the fence was lined with barbed wire. If he tried to get over the fence, he'd be a perfect target for the Germans behind him.

Running in a panic, he suddenly heard Peter's voice call out, "Over here!"

The boy had escaped without much difficulty because he knew the yard like the back of his hand. Now he was sitting on the outside of the fence, holding up the bottom, waiting for the others to come.

Blankers made a quick dive for it. Out of the corner of his eye he could just see Dijkmans coming. When he was through he turned around to look and saw Cor approaching too, his left arm limp by his side.

Dijkmans made it through easily. At that moment, something seemed to confuse the Germans; briefly, they turned aside their searchlights and hesitated.

It was all the time Cor needed to slip through the escape hatch. His injured arm was so painful that he had to bite his tongue to keep himself quiet.

"What happened to the others?" Peter asked.

"Meijer has been hit," Cor panted hoarsely. "Willem was under the car and probably headed out in another direction. I haven't seen Heins."

The boy hesitated, wanting to give Heins a chance. "Heins, where are you? Get over here!" shouted Blankers at the top of his voice. He realized that he was drawing the Germans' attention, but he couldn't just leave Heins alone to fend for himself.

"I'm coming!" The voice seemed to come from close by. At the same moment, the Germans opened fire again. Heins ran as fast as he could to the hole in the fence, chased by a hail of bullets. Dijkmans and Blankers returned fire to give Heins some cover. Almost miraculously, Heins managed to get through the hole unharmed. Then they crawled through the bushes away from the fence. Not until they were at least twenty metres away from the fence did they dare to jump up and run off.

This wasn't the end of it, of course. The Germans might decide to pursue them.

Peter led the way because he was the one who knew the territory. The sky had become a bit lighter, so they could see where they were going. Suddenly, a dark figure loomed in front of them.

Panic! How did a German get ahead of them?

Then they heard Willem's voice. "It's only me, boys; relax."

As they quickly made their way down the railway tracks, they exchanged bits of information. Willem had known he couldn't possibly reach the hole in the fence. When he noticed that all the German sentries had gone off in pursuit of the men heading for the fence, he had simply walked out through the deserted gate. That's how he had gotten ahead of them.

Before he had boldly walked out of the exit, Willem had heard a German soldier declare Meijer dead. That's what the men had been afraid of; now they were sure. It was a crushing blow.

But they weren't at all safe yet; although they heard no more shooting, there was a hubbub of a different kind–a number of different vehicles were being started up.

They trotted along the railway. They passed the place where they had fixed the derailers. It was very likely now that the Germans would find the devices.

A little farther they turned left and headed across the field. Aided by Blankers, Cor had wrapped a handkerchief and a scarf around his injured arm.

As they were walking, Blankers noticed that the wind had turned to the west. It wasn't so cold anymore. The snow on the ground was becoming wet and sticking to their shoes; this was a sure sign of thaw. It didn't make the going any easier, though.

They were completely out of breath when they finally reached the old mill where they had left the scow. They quickly got in and started punting for all they were worth.

Seven had left on the mission, but only six returned. That one terrible thought wouldn't leave them alone. Meijer was dead. They had tried too much this time.

Willem, especially, was plagued by doubt and self-reproach. As leader, he should have known better!

Blankers had other misgivings; had they done right? Shouldn't they instead have waited for God to bring deliverance in His own time? Why didn't they use prayer, that most powerful of weapons?

This was not the first time Blankers had been plagued by doubts, but the feeling was especially acute now because one of his friends had died in battle. But as always he concluded, "I can and may not act otherwise!" Freedom was at stake, and more than just national liberty. This was a struggle for the freedom to serve God according to His Word. Many people had fought and died for that cause during the eighty-year-war of Dutch independence from Spain more than three centuries earlier. German national socialism was an evil power that had to be resisted. It was resistance sanctioned by the crown and by the legally elected Dutch government. Prince Bernhard himself was commander-in-chief of the Dutch armed forces to which Blankers and his friends also belonged. Meijer had laid down his life for a just cause, a cause for which many others had given their lives, including the thousands of Allied soldiers fighting and dying in the Ardennes at that very moment.

The men took turns punting again, and presently they passed under the viaduct. Just a few minutes and they would be home.

Suddenly, far off in the distance, an immense flame shot up into the sky. A second later, a tremendous blast split the silence of the night. Large chunks of wood and steel flew hundreds of metres into the air. The echo of the blast reverberated for several seconds.

Darkness once again closed in, but the men had the satisfaction of knowing that their labours had not been entirely in vain. It would take the enemy days, possibly even weeks, to repair all the intricate trestle work of the railway bridge. That delay could become important.

They hastily punted on. The sooner they were inside, the safer they would be.

At last the men secured the scow and silently slipped back to the inn. Peter said goodbye and left. He would have no trouble reaching the farmhouse where he and the rest of his family had found temporary lodging. Willem tried to praise the boy highly, but the slightly embarrassed Peter shrugged off the thanks. The rest of the men disappeared inside the inn. The minute they were in, the door was locked and bolted.

The innkeeper's wife, who hadn't slept a wink all night, was with them at once. She took them into a dimly lit room, gave them something warm to drink, and rebandaged Cor's arm. The wound was fairly ugly; Cor would need a doctor for it. For the time being, she was concerned with disinfecting the arm and stopping the bleeding.

Going back to the city would mean some danger. They wanted to leave immediately but then decided to wait until curfew lifted. They would try to get out before the first light of dawn, hoping to do so without leaving a trail.

The fact that the weather had changed would help. The west wind usually brought a thick cloud cover and rain. Rain would take care of their tracks in the snow.

Even though their mission, the destruction of the railway bridge, had been a success, the men felt depressed over the death of their comrade-in-arms.

Their hasty flight had forced them to abandon the rest of their equipment and a supply of explosives in the railroad yard. They took what was left in the van and hid it in the inn. Probably the local resistance unit would be able to make good use of it. In any event, it was far too risky to take the stuff back in the van.

The minute curfew was lifted, they said goodbye to the hospitable wife of the innkeeper. Willem and Blankers got in the front while the others jumped in the back. Because Cor was painfully injured, Willem would do the driving.

It was still completely dark outside, and that was to their advantage. The Germans might try to set up roadblocks here and there, but they wouldn't be able to organize a thorough search until the first light of day.

It was drizzling. The snow quickly changed into a slushy mess. Willem didn't dare take the highway but instead threaded his way down narrow, winding country roads full of potholes and puddles. He had to use all his wits to keep from careening into a ditch. Only a few kilometres from the city, Willem headed for an isolated farm whose owner was an old acquaintance and a true patriot. It was too light to go on; they had to find out whether the access roads to the city were being watched.

The farmer was happy to see them. Immediately, he called a few people he knew could be trusted. To any uninformed listener it sounded as if the farmer were only chatting about trivia. This was done in case the enemy was listening in on the telephone line.

Willem, who knew the code, heard his worst fears confirmed.
The Germans were indeed watching the roads and inspecting any and all vehicles going into the city. There was no way they could go on, at least not by car. Willem sat down to talk it over with the farmer. He agreed to hide the van in one of his barns for the time being. Once things cooled down, Willem could send someone to pick it up.

Willem and Blankers would go to the city on foot. Heins and Dijkmans agreed to do the same thing but by a different route. Cor's wound would arouse suspicions immediately, so it was agreed that he would stay on the farm for a while. Once back in the city, Willem would send a doctor out to the farm. Cor would try to make his way back into the city once the heat was off.

A half hour later Willem and Blankers started out with their collars turned up as protection against the biting wind. They struggled along at the side of the road. The water and the snow had already soaked through their shoes, numbing their feet.

A forty-five minute walk brought them to the outskirts of the city. There they were met by German soldiers and some Dutch policemen. All traffic was stopped and examined and car occupants interrogated. Cyclists and pedestrians were also questioned, but less severely.

"Keep your wits about you, Gerard," growled Willem. "The story is that we left early this morning to hunt for food." As part of their alibi, each carried a burlap bag with some cauliflower, onions, and turnips.

They were halted and told to show their identity papers. These were falsified, of course. Willem told the policeman a story about all the trouble they'd had that morning just to get a little bit of food.

The policeman was only half interested; he checked the contents of the bags, but he didn't confiscate them. It could have been a lot worse. He waved them on.

Relieved, the two men walked on toward the warehouse. When they finally arrived, they were totally exhausted. It had been a wild night, but at least they were still alive.

CHAPTER FIVE

OOM KOOS, THE PERFECT HOST

After that moderately successful strike, the weather changed again; it turned colder, with temperatures dipping below zero. Early one afternoon Blankers was walking through the nearly deserted city streets on his way back to the warehouse, having just delivered a package of forged identity cards.

Today he was in a relatively cheerful mood. The battle of the Ardennes had turned to the Allies' favour. The German advance had been halted, and now the Allies were steadily gaining ground.

Yesterday Blankers had been to church for the first time in weeks. The fact that the police had been fooled when they examined his identity papers had given him enough courage to accompany the elderly Gerritsens. For the first time in many weeks, he had actually enjoyed a Sunday.

Going to church was not without its perils, but no one was entirely safe nowadays.

The Germans still suspected that the terrorists came from the city. The derailer had been discovered and removed before a train had come, but beyond that the Germans hadn't been able to find any trace of the escaped saboteurs. But during the past few days, they had carried out numerous raids on various houses around the city. Up until now all the members of the resistance unit had managed to escape attention, and not a single German had yet visited the warehouse. But the threat of a raid and a search remained imminent.

Lost in thought, Blankers hurried home. Before he knew it he was entering the narrow alleyway between the two tall buildings. He rapped the code signal on the metal door.

Seconds later the bolt slid aside in response. Blankers opened the door and entered the courtyard.

Just then a German military van came racing into the alleyway. Blankers couldn't shut the door fast enough and walk on. The van screamed into the courtyard, and after it halted abruptly, its occupants jumped out. Before he realized what was going on, Blankers was surrounded by a German non-com and five privates.

The non-com pointed to the door of the warehouse and snarled, "*Aufmachen! Schnell!*[2]"

What could he do? Desperately he tried to think of something that would delay them and give Gerritsen time to plan. But he couldn't think of anything. And what did it matter anyway? There was so much contraband material in the warehouse—things like weapons, explosives, sabotage supplies, a printing press, a radio transmitter, and a clearinghouse for false identity papers. If these Germans tried, they could find plenty.

The soldiers shoved him toward the warehouse door. Just as Blankers was about to slip the key into the lock, Gerritsen opened the door from the inside. He had heard the van drive up and watched what was going on through one of the windows.

Gerritsen put on his most engaging smile and nodded at the Germans. "Please come in," he said breezily. "Ah, Gerard, back already? Why don't you sweep up."

Blankers' mouth dropped open. Had the old man lost his marbles? Gerritsen was acting as if he had invited the Germans for tea! Obviously, however, the old man was acting. He must be planning to fool them.

But what could his plan be? Blankers couldn't follow it. The only thing clear to him was that he was being treated as a warehouse assistant. Dutifully, he took one of the corn-brooms hanging from the wall and began to sweep the floor. It was a good thing he could keep his hands busy because they were shaking.

Gerritsen paid no more attention to him and turned instead to the non-com, who was just as perplexed as Blankers was.

---

[2] Open up! Hurry!

"You're here for a bottle of wine or some schnapps," he said warmly, his smile almost comical. "I'm really sorry, but it's almost all gone." Broadly gesturing at the kegs stacked up along the wall, he added, "Those crates are nearly all empty!" Then he said, almost conspiratorially, "But I have one keg of brandy left. Excellent quality! You may want to buy that . . . But you should try it first."

The soldiers didn't remember their orders saying anything about brandy. They were told to search the warehouse because an informer had claimed that something was very wrong here. But the word "schnapps" triggered something in their brains, and the friendly old man's generous offer couldn't be refused. That wouldn't be polite! There was no harm in tasting some of the Dutchman's brandy. So, seduced by the idea of a free drink, they followed Gerritsen.

The old man calmly walked up to a keg, pulled out the plug, and inserted a wooden tap. That was not done without spilling a bit of the precious liquid, however, and the soldiers sniffed eagerly. Gerritsen fetched a measuring glass, opened the tap, half filled the glass, and held it out to the non-com, who drank it down greedily. Eyes bulging and tongues almost hanging out of their mouths, the privates looked on. Then one of them spotted more glasses and a pitcher standing on a table nearby. One of the more aggressive soldiers seized a glass, pushed Gerritsen away from the keg, and helped himself. The rest of them quickly followed suit.

Gerritsen protested weakly. "But Herr Unteroffizier, that's not what I had intended. It's the last I've got. I must ask you to pay!"

The German grinned and chortled, "*Schon gut, schon gut.*[3]" Then he helped himself again.

Soon Gerritsen and Blankers had lost count of the number of drinks the Germans were putting away. Blankers had first looked on in disgust, but now he realized what the old man was up to. He swept the floor and watched from a distance.

---

[3] All right, all right.

36

Grateful for the old man's helpless generosity, the Germans decided they might as well go all out. They took some kegs down from the wall, positioned them around the brandy keg, and sat down. Pretty soon they were in the best of spirits, laughing, joking, and conveniently forgetting all about their assignment.

Gerritsen had apparently resigned himself to it. He sat down next to the non-com, who was really beginning to relax.

The brandy loosened the officer's tongue. He told Gerritsen he'd been ordered to search the warehouse. "*Nein*," it was all nonsense, the Krieg was lost anyway. But the schnapps "*Ist gut*," and his generous host was indeed "*ein freundlich Hollander!*[4]"

---

[4] a friendly Dutchman

After about an hour or so of partying, it finally began to occur to his soggy brain that this couldn't go on. He managed to hoist himself up and shouted to his soldiers, "*Aufhoren! Haussuche!*[5]"

Laughing, he slapped Gerritsen on the shoulders and mumbled apologetically, "*Befehl ist Befehl!*[6]"

Blankers, who was still poking around with the broom in his hand, had placed a couple of crates and kegs on top of the trapdoor leading into the cellar. He still was scared. If the Germans were going to take their "*Haussuche*" seriously, they'd find everything.

Gerritsen remained calm and paid no attention to Blankers. He accompanied the soldiers as they made their way between the rows of kegs and occasionally rapped against one of them to prove that they were all empty. In the meantime, he kept up an animated discussion with the befuddled non-com, who seemed perfectly satisfied that his host was "clean."

Then they came to the staircase leading up. The non-com took one look at it and felt something beginning to heave inside his stomach. He didn't like the looks of that staircase at all! In fact, he suddenly didn't like the whole warehouse anymore, the way it was twirling and whirling.

"*Schon gut!*[7]" he blurted, and he swung his arm back to give his generous host yet another slap on the back. Fortunately, the obliging Gerritsen moved within range to prevent the non-com from making a complete fool of himself. Herr Unteroffizier informed him that the warehouse would get a clean bill of health!

The old man escorted his happy guests to the front door. The non-com was particularly friendly to his host, and he assured him that he would come back some day. That was the kind of promise that Gerritsen could have done without!

---

[5] That's enough! Search the house!

[6] An order is an order!

[7] All right!

The whole gang swaggered toward the van and managed to clamber into it after a couple of near falls. They turned the van around with great difficulty and successfully squeezed into the alley. Right at the end of the alley, just as the van was about to turn into the street, part of the right rear fender and the back bumper were rearranged by a brick wall. Then the van lurched forward out into the street, leaving Gerritsen and Blankers to muse about the dangerous consequences, behind a securely locked door. Together they walked back into the warehouse. Mrs. Gerritsen came down the staircase to join them.

She had heard every word but had wisely kept out of sight.

Tante Miep looked pale, but she was also very calm. Blankers felt a deep admiration for this elderly couple who could stare danger in the face and still make such fools of the Germans.

Gerritsen explained that that was exactly what the keg of brandy was for. Oom Koos wasn't particulary proud of the fact that he had tricked those young men into getting drunk, but it had served a good purpose. But suppose they had declined his generous offer? Suppose there had been a couple among, them who didn't drink alcohol? It had been a close call.

Those six drunks would probably end up in jail or with extra KP duties, but the people who had made out the orders would undoubtedly send other soldiers!

Before that happened, the warehouse had to be made safe. After a brief discussion with his wife, Gerritsen decided to warn Willem, who could then also alert the others. For the time being, nobody should come anywhere near the warehouse. Oom Koos and Blankers would quickly move whatever looked suspicious to the secret cellar. The trapdoor would have to be made invisible. Tante Miep put her coat on and left. When the alley door was securely locked behind her, Gerritsen and Blankers got to work. They filled a number of empty kegs with weapons and explosives and lugged them into the cellar.

At last all the contraband stuff had vanished. After a final inspection, the two men locked the trapdoor. They slid a large, square, concrete trough over it. Normally this container would be used to prepare large quantities of raspberries or other fruit for preserves.

They filled the container full of water and dumped a few armloads of dirty burlap bags into it. The bags needed to soak before they could be washed and dried. That was the impression they hoped to give to any unwelcome visitor who might come calling.

By now everything looked very innocent. The concrete container looked like a permanent fixture, and there was nothing to indicate that there was a secret trapdoor under it.

Gerritsen nodded and smiled warmly. "I think it'll work, Gerard. That is, unless we're dealing with treason. If so, then nothing will work. It seems to me you had better disappear for a while, somewhere really safe. Willem will know of a place for you."

Blankers wouldn't hear of that. He wanted to stay with the brave elderly couple as long as possible. If necessary, he could always make his escape across the rooftops. Gerritsen didn't agree with him but finally yielded.

Tante Miep came back and told them that she had located Willem. He would make sure that none of the resistance people visited the warehouse in the coming days.

By now it was evening; the three of them went upstairs to have supper. That night Gerritsen's prayer was more urgent than ever before. They all felt completely dependent on God's mercy.

After supper they chatted for a while by the flickering light of a single candle. There were no Germans to be seen in the courtyard. Finally they decided to go to bed. Blankers didn't bother to undress and couldn't sleep well. Repeatedly he was jolted out of his slumber, thinking he had heard something. Several times he tiptoed into the living room to have a look outside.

The German raid didn't take place that night. In the morning Blankers sensed that Oom Koos and Tante Miep had slept much better than he had. After breakfast he took his usual position by the window. The day dragged on. Blankers still feared that the Germans would come, but sometimes he found himself almost wishing for it. If it was going to happen anyway, better get it over with! But the day was utter boredom.

Night fell at last. Feeling calmer than he had the previous night, Blankers put on his pyjamas. He was asleep almost immediately and didn't wake up until the alarm clock went off at seven o'clock the next morning.

He was relieved to discover that once again nothing had happened. Well, maybe they had seen the worst of it.

He quickly got dressed and went to have breakfast. Tante Miep was already up getting everything ready.

Then a car wheeled loudly into the alley and stopped in front of the alley door. Searchlights penetrated the early morning mist. A horn blared and a voice barked, *"Aufmachen, Polizei!*[8]*"*

---

[8] Open up, police!

CHAPTER SIX

A ROOFTOP DASH FOR FREEDOM

Half scared out of his wits, Blankers stared out the window. The van waited outside the warehouse. From the reflection of the headlights on the steel door, he could just make out the uniforms of the dreaded Green Police. He knew that these men were much more sinister than ordinary Wehrmacht soldiers. They wouldn't be as easy as the last bunch.

Gerritsen and his wife had come in. They were both ashen faced but completely in control of themselves.

"This is it, Gerard," Gerritsen said. "Take to the roofs. You know the way."

Still Blankers hesitated. Could he leave these two people to face this ordeal all by themselves?

The pounding became more persistent. The Green Police didn't like to be kept waiting.

The old man insisted. "You can't stay here! They're already looking for you. If they catch you now, they'll recognize you for sure, and your life won't be worth a cent. Wait till I'm downstairs. They'll go into the warehouse, and then you can make your escape unseen."

He shoved Blankers into the bedroom and headed downstairs.

Blankers no longer hesitated; Gerritsen was right. He dressed quickly, gathered his few possessions, and shoved them into his pockets. Then he grabbed his overcoat and headed for the closet.

Outside, the Germans were hammering away at the door with their rifle butts. They were screaming angrily now. They quieted down as Gerritsen walked across the courtyard and called, "I'm coming!"

Tante Miep followed Blankers into his bedroom. She was terribly concerned about her husband but perhaps even more about Blankers. "You go out onto the ledge, Gerard, and then wait a couple of seconds. I'll bolt the door behind you."

Blankers walked through the clothes closet and opened the trapdoor to the outside. "Goodbye, Tante Miep," he said softly. "I hope God will protect you and your husband."

"We're always safe with Him," she replied simply. Though there were tears in her eyes, her voice was steady, full of conviction.

Blankers slid back the two bolts of the little trapdoor and opened it to the outside. He stooped down and swung out onto the wide ledge. Quickly Tante Miep pulled the door shut and bolted it.

The cutting January wind lashed Blankers' face. Somewhere downstairs, Gerritsen said calmly, "I've got to get dressed first; I didn't expect anybody at this hour of the day!"

A German voice retorted angrily. In the meantime, the car had been driven into the courtyard and its headlights turned off.

Blankers waited for just a moment yet; the voices had almost reached the warehouse door.

In the clear now, he carefully inched his way to the end of the ledge. At this point he had to cross over to a second ledge. The courtyard was directly below him. In the sparse light of early dawn, he could see the outlines of the van below.

What if the driver was still in it? If he was and happened to look up, he would spot Blankers right away. Up here he was a sitting duck.

Blankers forcibly put that thought aside in order to concentrate on his precarious path. A thin sheet of ice on the ledge made the going very tricky. If he fell from this height, he probably wouldn't survive.

Carefully, tensely, he made his way along the ledge. The ledge had been built well. It would hold his weight.

Behind him the noises were indistinct. They all must be inside the warehouse. The second ledge ended at a flat roof. Once he set foot on that, he breathed a sigh of relief. The worst was behind him.

The flat roof was covered with gravel that crunched under his feet. If there were people inside, they would surely hear him.

He made a wide detour around a couple of skylights. Then he came to the end of the roof. Beyond him was a chasm about two metres wide and no less than eighteen metres deep. On the other side of it was the flat roof of another warehouse.

He suddenly recalled that there was supposed to be a board around here that he could use as a bridge. He found the board, which was sturdy enough, but icy. Blankers couldn't muster the courage to walk across it. Only three paces separated him from the next roof, but he was sure that if he set foot on the board, he would slip and fall.

What was he to do? He couldn't very well stay here, and the way back was cut off. For a moment he considered crawling across the board, but that was too risky.

Then he had an idea. He brushed away the layer of gravel on the roof and found a layer of coarse sand beneath. He took a couple of handfuls and dusted the icy plank with it. Once he knew that his footing was secure, Blankers was across in a moment.

The rest was child's play; he knew that at the end of the second roof a wooden staircase led the way down.

When he got half way down the staircase, he spotted a couple of workmen walking through the alley. He waited motionless until they passed. Within seconds he was down on the ground.

He had made it! Deep relief engulfed him. But that didn't last long. He thought of the elderly couple back in the warehouse. What would become of them? If the Green Police happened to find the hiding place with all the contraband material, they would almost surely be shot, perhaps right then and there to terrorize the rest of the members of the Resistance. That happened quite commonly these days.

Glancing around, Blankers walked out into the street. There wasn't a single German in sight! But he suspected that the Germans might have posted a couple of lookouts he couldn't see.

He pulled his hat down over his eyes, turned up his collar, and leaned nonchalantly against a warehouse wall. From here he could keep his eye on the alley that led to the Gerritsen warehouse. The Germans were still there, and when they left they would most probably come out this way.

Blankers waited and waited; at least half an hour went by. He was getting chilled to the bone, but he simply had to know what had happened.

Everything remained quiet; apparently nobody else had noticed the early morning raid. An occasional cyclist or pedestrian went by, but nobody paid any attention to the man leaning against the warehouse.

A bell chimed, the only one in town that hadn't been appropriated by the Germans for their munitions factories. Blankers discovered that he had been standing there for an hour and a half. He could hardly resist the urge to walk into the alleyway to look. It was hazardous, he had to admit, but this waiting around was driving him crazy.

He was spared the trouble when he suddenly saw the German van emerge from the alley. Blankers hid around the corner. There he waited, watched, and listened. Would the van come this way?

A split second later, it drove past. Blankers got only a glance, but what he saw turned his heart to stone. Up front, between two uniformed Germans, sat Oom Koos.

It was as if his whole world collapsed. All their attempts to cover their tracks had been in vain! Blankers fought back tears of bitterness and regret. He felt ashamed that he had abandoned the couple, even though common sense told him he couldn't have helped at all.

Blankers knew what he had to do. He had to go to the warehouse to find out what happened. He had to find out if there were any hope.

It was perilous. He had no idea whether any of the Germans had been left behind. After a successful raid, they often left a few men to watch the place and to seize anybody who showed up. A lot of Resistance members had been caught that way.

Maybe they were waiting for him even now. But he had to do it. He had to know.

He hurried toward the alley. If any Germans were posted at the warehouse, he would simply pretend to be Gerard de Wit, a warehouse employee. He might get away with it.

Soon he found himself in the alley walking toward the courtyard.

The metal door was still open; how should he interpret that? Was that a good sign or not? He didn't know.

Come on, he scolded himself, any hesitancy now will almost certainly arouse suspicion!

Nonchalantly, he walked through the door and went toward the warehouse.

The door had been closed but was not locked. He lifted the latch and went inside.

It took him a minute to adjust to the darkness. He was astonished at what he saw. The crates and kegs and various pieces of equipment were thrown all over the place. Most had been destroyed. The place was in a shambles. But Blankers didn't care about that; there was only one thing that interested him. He hurried over to the large concrete container.

What he saw pleased him immensely. The container was exactly where he and Gerritsen had put it, and when he came closer, he saw that it was still filled with water and wet burlap bags.

So their headquarters had not been discovered! Suddenly Blankers felt like singing and shouting! He charged toward the staircase and went up three steps at a time.

The second story, too, was in chaos, but he didn't care and continued climbing until he got to the attic.

Then a new fear constricted his throat. Everything was so deathly quiet. Had they taken Tante Miep too? Throwing caution to the wind, he ran across the attic floor to the living room door. Briefly, he hesitated. Could it be a trap?

46

But when he flung the door open, he saw Tante Miep sitting all alone in the living room. In front of her, lying on the table, was an open Bible. She had been crying. But her face broke into a smile when she saw Blankers come into the room.

"Gerard, is that you? It's a good thing they didn't get you! But I think it's very careless of you to come back."

"What happened to Oom Koos?" Blankers asked excitedly.

"They took him for questioning. He may be home soon because they didn't find anything suspicious."

The words were calmly chosen and spoken, but there was a slight tremor in the woman's voice. Blankers could well understand; Tante Miep was acting pretty spunky, but she was worried. What would happen to her husband who was now being interrogated, and possibly even abused, by the sinister Secret Police?

Now she told the story; Oom Koos had received the Germans with his perfect calm and self-assuredness. They had searched everything, even inspecting the concrete container and removing some of the wet burlap bags, but it had never occurred to them to look under the container.

Failing to find anything and unable to get Gerritsen to speak, they became more and more angry. They ransacked the upstairs, including Blankers' bedroom, but they hadn't even found the emergency exit in the clothes closet! If they had found it, Gerritsen would have tried to convince them that it was simply a fire escape.

They left in frustration, taking Gerritsen with them. He had protested loudly but hadn't resisted.

Now Blankers felt both relieved and defeated. He was immensely grateful that they hadn't found the cellar but upset because they had taken his friend away for questioning. He tried to comfort Tante Miep to the best of his ability, but he quickly discovered that the woman needed less comforting than he did, although she had been crying earlier. She really knew what her only comfort in life and death was.

At first she tried to persuade Blankers to leave, but he flatly refused. He wasn't about to leave her alone in this chaos.

He went back downstairs and worked like a slave to get everything back in its place. By the time Tante Miep called him up for lunch, most of the mess on the warehouse floor had been cleaned up.

After lunch he attacked the second story, which was even worse than the warehouse floor. He laboured and sweated all afternoon, so that by supper time, things were fairly orderly. By now he was dog tired and all his joints were aching, but the hard work had eased his panic about Oom Koos. Tante Miep also had worked hard at bringing the living quarters back to normal.

After supper they sat and chatted. They still hoped that Gerritsen would return before nightfall, but when curfew came, they knew he would not return so soon.

They discussed the war. To Blankers' amazement, Mrs. Gerritsen talked about the Germans without a trace of bitterness or hatred in her voice. She reminded him that Germans are no greater sinners than anyone else. Many of them were seduced and misled because they had grown up in the devilish doctrine of national socialism, and others fought simply because they had no choice.

In theory Blankers agreed, but sometimes his hatred of German terrorism made him bitter. Still, this kind of chat with Tante Miep did him a lot of good. He needed to be reminded of the truth once in a while. Her husband had been carted off by the Germans, but there was no hatred in her voice. She believed that this war was a chastening of God because the nations had forgotten about Him. "Pray God, that he may ease you, His Gospel be your cure" were the words that the author of the "Wilhelmus"[9] had put into the mouth of Prince William of Orange in a different time of war and persecution. These words were valid even now. The elderly woman understood that, and this understanding enabled her to bear her burdens without complaining.

He had to focus on that himself, Blankers realized. He resolved to ask God to keep him from sinful hatred.

---

[9] the Dutch national anthem, composed in the sixteenth century in honour of William of Orange (William the Silent).

At ten o'clock he went to his room; before he went to bed, he submitted all his needs and his sinfulness to his heavenly Father. He fervently prayed for God to be merciful to the oppressed and to bring deliverance soon. He also prayed for Gerritsen and for his own wife and children, whom he had not seen for such a long time.

With prayer came peace; the dark thoughts that had been haunting his heart gave way to new hope and courage. Then he lay down, tuning in to the monotonous melody played by the wind, a melody that gradually grew to a mighty crescendo as a storm developed. Before long, Blankers lapsed into a deep, dreamless sleep.

CHAPTER SEVEN

ON THE RUN AGAIN!

Two days passed–long, gloomy days for Tante Miep and her guest. Constantly they looked out the window, wishing for Gerritsen's return.

What had happened to him? After all, the Germans had no evidence against him. They had no reason to hold him!

Blankers had to keep reminding himself that the Germans needed no evidence. They could execute people on mere suspicion. Maybe they had already done that to Oom Koos.

Blankers was itching to see if he could pick up some information, but that would be foolhardy. Probably the warehouse was still under surveillance. If he went out now, he would almost certainly be followed.

Willem and the others didn't show up. They would wait to make sure that the Germans no longer suspected the warehouse.

During the afternoon of the second day following the arrest, somebody banged on the courtyard door.

Blankers dashed over to the window and was thrilled to see Oom Koos standing in the alley.

Never before had "Gerard" been so quick to open the door! Seconds later the old man was upstairs, locked in his wife's loving embrace.

Gerritsen looked tired, but his eyes were keen and laughing. He told them he'd been questioned twice during the past two days but that the Germans hadn't gotten a thing out of him. In desperation they had finally charged him with slipping drinks to right-minded German soldiers. But Gerritsen had insisted that the right-minded German soldiers had gotten drunk on their own, despite his protests. The valiant old man had even demanded payment for his losses! No matter how much they had threatened him, Gerritsen had kept calm. In the end they had concluded that the old man was totally harmless. They had released him, and in less than an hour, he was home.

That evening was unlike any celebration before! Tante Miep even dipped into her sparse reserves of food and extras. There wasn't much to go around. Before the war they could have thrown a real party, but this wasn't before the war. And even so, they were well off, certainly much better than people in the large cities of the western provinces. Those people were very hungry.

However modest the meal, it somehow seemed better than any other, simply because it was spiced with so much human happiness!

Blankers was reminded of the time several months earlier when he had unexpectedly dropped in on his wife and children. That had been a happy night too. But that visit had been ruined by a German raid that made him a captive.

He had been rescued and was still very thankful for that. And yet memories of that night intensified his yearning for home. He was happy and sad at the same time, although he was careful not to let his sadness show.

They discussed the future. One thing was sure, they wouldn't be able to use the warehouse in the near future. Once the Germans smelled prey, they would hunt that quarry down without fail. Another raid could come at any time, and if the trapdoor were ever discovered, everything would be over.

The Resistance would have to find another base. Gerritsen and his wife were quite prepared to sacrifice their lives for the good cause, but to continue using the warehouse as a base would be pointless and stupid.

They might soon have an opportunity to transfer all the supplies elsewhere. But before anything could be decided, they had to consult with Willem.

Blankers decided to slip out the next day to see if he could contact Willem. He would have to be doubly careful now, in case he was followed. It wouldn't be easy, but they had no choice.

They went to bed early that night; Gerritsen needed extra rest to recover form his ordeal.

Blankers couldn't sleep right away. Various plans raced through his head. He was sure that he could not stay here any longer. The warehouse was probably being watched. It would be too dangerous, not just for himself, but also for Oom Koos and Tante Miep. If he was to continue working for the Resistance, he'd have to find another hideout.

The next day was a typical cold winter day. He walked through deserted streets with an eye out for a follower. He didn't see anything suspicious, but just to be sure, he made several detours. Two or three times he quickly ducked into a side street and dashed down some alleys and fire routes in order to throw any possible pursuer off his trail. Finally, he got to Willem's hideout.

He found Heins and Dijkmans there too. The three men knew about Gerritsen's arrest, but they hadn't heard about his release yet.

They relaxed when they heard that Oom Koos had been turned loose, and they agreed unanimously that the usefulness of the warehouse had come to an end. They also agreed that "Gerard" had to find a new place to stay.

They discussed every possibility and every problem and finally decided that Willem would call on the farm where Cor was staying. It was only a couple of kilometres outside the city, so Willem agreed to go immediately. He would ask the farmer if Blankers could stay there also. He knew the man pretty well and was sure that he wouldn't refuse. Eventually the farm might even be used as new headquarters for the Underground, but that decision had to wait until later.

Blankers would report to the farmhouse the next day. In a sense he looked forward to it because it meant being outdoors again, and it also meant he would be able to join Cor, who was still recovering from the bullet wound in his arm. At the same time Blankers felt sad that he would have to leave those two dear old people and the trusty warehouse. He would never forget what they had done for him, and he would never be able to repay them. He resolved to visit them right after the war and to maintain close contact with them in the future.

After the war . . . When would that be?

Midafternoon he went back to the warehouse and informed the Gerritsen couple of the decision. They nodded their approval. They could well understand his leaving, but they were also sad about it. Having been through a lot together, the three had become very close. During supper that night Tante Miep treated Blankers a little bit with some extra food.

He was up early the next morning to say goodbye. After thanking them warmly for all they had done for him, he left.

Twenty minutes later he was out of the city and on a footpath that led through the open fields.

It was a surprisingly pleasant day. The sun shone cheerfully in a silvery grey sky, the wind blew out of the south, and there was a fragrance of spring in the air. Birds darted up and down across the fields, and in some places the grass was beginning to turn green.

Blankers had left the warehouse in rather sombre spirits, but the wide open spaces cheered him up. It was as if the balmy wind was busy blowing all the cobwebs out of his mind and replacing them with a spirit of hope. His step became jauntier as his eyes soaked up the beauty of the landscape.

Without a doubt, spring was coming. Could the liberation be far behind?

He began to sing some Psalms and patriotic songs until he suddenly stopped himself, a trifle embarrassed. Wasn't it unsuitable to be so happy when the world situation was so sad? But then he had to chuckle at his own foolishness. This beautiful promise of spring was a pure gift from God, the kind of gift to accept gratefully. And no matter what problems lie ahead, one may still sing to the glory of God!

He spotted the farm off in the distance and walked quickly toward it, anxious to see what was in store for him.   A man was out in the yard, apparently waiting for him. When Blankers got closer he saw that it was Cor. It was a happy reunion. Cor's arm was in a sling and recovering nicely. He had nothing but praise for the way he was being treated on the farm and was intensely happy that Gerard had come to join him.

Reassured by the warm welcome, Blankers accompanied his friend to the farmhouse.

CHAPTER EIGHT

THE SPECTRE OF STARVATION

Back in Blankers' village, very little had happened while he was gone. There was one big change. The nearest junior high school didn't reopen after the Christmas break due to a shortage of fuel. Jan Blankers (whose name was pronounced *yon*) and his friend Kris Kooiman had no school for the time being.

That didn't bother the boys much; those constant trips back and forth to the city school on their worn-out bikes had been a pain. Often they had arrived at school soaked to the skin and then had to spend the rest of the day in chilly classrooms. They were glad that that was over.

Christmas vacation had passed weeks ago; Jaap lived at the Kooiman farm and attended sixth grade in town. Jan stayed home to help his mother with the chores and do all kinds of little jobs around the house, mindful of his promise to help her.

He often hiked out to the farm to see Kris. There was usually something to do there—chores or games the boys could play in the barn. Jan enjoyed many meals over there, too. And the Kooimans always gave him some food for home: potatoes, turnips, a bag of peas, beans, or a sack of flour they had ground themselves. Once in a while they included a sausage or a chunk of bacon, but that didn't happen often since meat of any kind was getting scarce. Needless to say, Mrs. Blankers was always delighted with the gifts and wondered how she would have managed without them. The official rations were getting smaller by the day.

Despite their skimping, the poorest in this town were still much better off than hundreds of thousands of city people in the western provinces. Hunger was so bad out there that many were dying of starvation.

Each day thousands of people took to the road with bicycles, handcarts, or baby buggies. They all came from cities in the western provinces and were heading for the farms in search of food, in search of hope. Sometimes they paid with cash, but usually they would barter with sheets, clothes, jewelry, and anything else they had left.

As winter passed into spring, there was no relief for the starving, and their search for food took them farther and farther from their homes.

When they came as far as Jan's town, it meant they had been walking for days. At night they would bed down in sheds and even chicken coops, only to go on again the next day.

Although the Kooiman farm was rather isolated, it didn't escape the wanderers' quest. Kooiman found these people a real problem. He had no intention of charging high prices as many of the farmers did. He charged only reasonable prices or nothing at all. But he couldn't possibly please everybody.

Occasionally a whole company of these people would stay overnight in the barn. They told the Kooimans heartbreaking stories about the misery and terror in the cities. Most people were truly grateful for the help the Kooimans gave them, but occasionally men threatened to become violent unless the Kooimans gave them more food.

Sometimes the Kooimans were visited by people working the black market trade. They offered to buy any amount of food the Kooimans might have available so that they could resell the food for terribly high prices. Kooiman wanted nothing to do with these sharks and always kicked them out of the yard. There were quite a few of them, very often people who normally wouldn't have given into this sort of thing but for whom the temptations had been just too great. Kooiman stubbornly refused to do business with them even though some of their offers were very tempting!

There was no doubt that the war was slowly winding down. The Germans had been thrown back in the Ardennes and were now on the defensive virtually everywhere. The Allies were just waiting for the weather to clear before making a direct assault on the Third Reich.

Despite these hopeful signs, however, many Dutch people lived on the brink of disaster. Peace would come, that was sure enough. But the question was whether it would come soon enough to save the starving masses in the west. Furthermore, if the Germans made good their threat to flood the whole countryside, the destruction would be unthinkable.

These were the uncertainties that kept people fretting all the time. Never before had these people prayed and worried so much. Some worried, some prayed, and many did both.

German terrorism increased daily. Everywhere people were picked up and promptly shot. Mrs. Blankers lived in constant fear for her husband. The Germans and their helpers had redoubled their efforts to search out such men. Her husband might well have been arrested and killed long ago for all she knew. It had been months since they'd heard anything about him.

Jan had once asked Gerrit Greven whether he knew anything, but he didn't. He had other things to worry about. His own situation back in town was becoming worse. Most of the villagers hated him with a passion, still convinced that he was working for the Germans. Once somebody threw a brick through his window.

This hatred grieved the dealer, but he managed to control himself. If the people only knew what he had done for their cause and the risks he took!

The only ones who knew Greven's secret were the Kooimans and a couple of select men from the Resistance. Greven knew how important it was for him to remain chummy with the Germans, especially now.

The liberation was coming, that was clear; but it was also clear that there would be a lot of bloodshed before the end. The Germans were reinforcing their defenses everywhere. Dutch men and boys were pressed into the service of the German *Organisation Todt* to dig trenches and help erect antitank barriers. They were told to bring a shovel and report to a particular place where they would be expected to work for no pay, closely watched by German supervisors. To escape this fate, quite a few went into hiding or got medical leave. But most of the work draftees had neither the imagination nor courage to escape.

The Resistance wanted to know what kind of defenses the Germans were planning; to find out was Greven's new assignment.

This was probably the most difficult assignment the dealer had ever been given. It was complicated by the fact that his secret ally, the one German within the Ortskommandant's office who was prepared to help Greven, had been transferred. So he had to do it all by himself.

Accordingly, he had to make himself look even more servile and greedy than before. He went about buying up all kinds of merchandise for exorbitant prices in order to sell it to the Ortskommandant or other German soldiers who were always happy to have something extra when they went on furlough.

The whole business was very distasteful, but Greven had no choice. It was the only way he could ingratiate himself with the enemy. It gave him golden opportunities to find out things he would otherwise never hear about.

The Resistance had provided Greven with a miniature camera that could be strapped to his chest and operated by remote control from his trouser pocket. By simply tugging at his shirt a bit and simultaneously pressing a button in his pocket, he could take photographs. It worked well, but he carried with him the painful knowledge that if he were caught he would be shot as a spy. Yet he never complained or refused.

He was most annoyed by the fact that the obnoxious Jonas Krom had decided to become his friend. Jonas wasn't stupid enough to think that the Germans could win the war. And he realized full well that if the Germans came to a bad end, so would he. He began to cling more and more to Greven simply because the dealer was so much smarter than he was. Secretly he hoped that Greven would somehow be able to take care of him once the Germans were no longer there to protect him.

Greven had insulted Jonas a couple of times in an effort to get rid of him, but Krom wasn't easily discouraged. Greven had to be careful not to be too obvious about it. That might make him suspect. In a way it was good to find out what the cowardly Krom was up to. After carefully weighing the pros and cons, Greven decided to put up with his presence.

As German atrocities intensified, there came some hopeful news about the war.

With the advent of spring, the Allied armies were on the move again. On the eastern front the Russians had unleashed an incredible winter offensive. At the beginning of February, the Red Army reached the Oder River, a hundred kilometres east of Berlin. They crossed the river and headed straight for the capital. In the meantime, a number of German armies were digging in around the city in a last desperate effort to halt the Russian offensive.

On the western front hostilities also resumed. During the first week of February, more than two thousand Allied bombers and fighter planes pounded German armies east of the city of Nijmegen. On the eighth of February, the English and Canadians opened their spring offensive. The Germans had cut the dikes on the south side of the Waal and Rhine rivers. Sometimes Allied soldiers had to wade chest deep through the water. In other places the spring thaw had turned the ground into sticky, heavy mud. Nevertheless, the offensives were successful, and by the twelfth of February, the German armies had retreated into their own forests.

But success was followed by failure. The long-expected offensive was stopped by mud and flooding. The rivers had swollen enormously. Eight kilometres of the road between Nijmegen and Kleef—the only supply line available—were covered by sixty centimetres of water. Hitler was defending himself with panzer divisions and paratroopers, most of them fanatical S.S troops grimly determined to fight to the bitter end.

The Allies tried to make a breakthrough because they wanted to cross the Rhine as soon as possible. But after ten days of hard fighting, they could manage only six kilometres.

Hitler had expressly forbidden his soldiers to retreat. Anybody caught retreating would be shot on the spot. They were also forbidden to surrender. If a soldier ran out of ammunition, he was expected to fight on with hand grenades, bayonet, or if necessary, his bare hands. Such were the decrees of the German fuhrer, who wouldn't risk his own safety at the front but manipulated things from his underground bunker in Berlin! Incredible as it may seem, his slaves obeyed.

To the Allies it seemed as if a steel door had been slammed shut in front of them. But they knew they had to reopen that door and also sensed that Hitler had few, if any, reserves to throw into the fray.

With each day the liberation came nearer, but it came painfully slow. In the western provinces, people had been reduced to eating tulip bulbs, sugar beets, and things even less appetizing. Central food administrations tried to dole out a half litre of watery soup per person per day, but sometimes even that wasn't available. Those most vulnerable, such as elderly people and small children, sometimes dropped dead right in the middle of the street. The number of deaths increased so quickly that there wasn't enough wood for caskets.

The northern provinces tried to come to the rescue of the western provinces, where 3.5 million people tottered on the edge of starvation. In the province of Groningen, barges were loaded up with potatoes, peas, and beans, but the Germans refused to let them go. The Dutch were being punished for their resistance to the illustrious Third Reich. The Germans had long maintained that the food supply to the western provinces would be restored the minute the striking railway workers went back to work. As long as the strike was on, there would be no food!

In addition to hunger, there was the cold. Fortunately the winter hadn't been especially severe, but even ordinary cold was too much for the ill-clad, starving people in the west. There was no longer any coal. It was every man for himself, as hordes of people went around stealing gates and balconies and cutting down trees in the parks and along the streets. Whole woods and public parks disappeared during the days of early spring 1945. The people needed fuel, both to keep warm and to cook their meagre supply of food. Burning useful and beautiful things in secret was a necessary evil. Fuel, like food, was one of the essentials of life.

The only ones with an abundance of both food and fuel were the Germans. They had hoarded huge quantities of both and would easily outlive the pitiful Hollanders scrounging about in the streets for scraps.

Surely liberation was just around the corner. But so was death, the Grim Reaper. For months the people wondered which would get to them first . . .

CHAPTER NINE

THE ALLIES CROSS THE RHINE!

Kooiman was glad that he had put away a decent supply of peat the previous year. During the summer it had been out in the field drying, and later it had been transferred to the barn. Mrs. Blankers and a few other needy people had been given their share of the supply. Kooiman had also cut down a number of trees in the Wilds. The farm was surviving the winter well. Although it was a fairly mild winter, it passed too slowly. One day in early March, Kooiman went out to check his fields. The ground was no longer frozen, but it wasn't dry enough to plough. It still needed a couple of nice days with warm sunshine and a fresh wind.

He was looking forward to spring. A lot had to be done before the land was all ploughed and seeded, and although Jan and Kris could help, Kooiman had to do most of it himself. Time was essential because anything could happen at any time that might prevent him from doing his farm chores.

If hostilities broke out here, Allied tanks might churn across his fields and ruin all his seed. Nevertheless, the ploughing and seeding had to be done. A farmer couldn't stop to consider the chances of war. There is always a need for food.

Though Kooiman was a farmer to the core, his thoughts kept drifting off to the front lines. The BBC had announced that the Americans were about to take Cologne. Unfortunately, Cologne was on the west bank of the Rhine. And it was really the Rhine that was holding the Allies back. It hadn't been breached in a single place.

Deep in thought, Kooiman walked back to the farmhouse. As he came into the yard, he spotted Greven cycling toward him, pedalling like a madman. Slightly amused, Kooiman watched Greven bounce across the yard, his short legs pumping very fast. Obviously excited, Greven jumped down from his bike and rushed up to the farmer. Grinning from ear to ear, he blurted, "They made it!"

"Who, where?" demanded Kooiman. He had a hunch but didn't dare say it.

"They crossed the Rhine!"

"Are you serious? That's terrific!"

They walked into the kitchen and joined Mrs. Kooiman. Greven explained how he knew. He was in good company now, and there was no longer any need for secrecy.

"Just an hour ago I was at the Ortskommandant's. He was listening to the radio with a very despondent look on his face. He hardly even noticed me come in.

"He was listening to the news reports in German. At first I thought he was listening to one of his own stations, but then it suddenly occurred to me that he had secretly tuned into an English broadcast in the German language! I knew that the Germans do that quite regularly because they don't trust their own news, but I was very surprised he didn't turn it off when I came in!

"It didn't take me long to find out why. And I can tell you that the Ortskommandant was pretty upset by the report. The announcer said that the Americans had made a quick dash for the Rhine. Near the town of Remagen, that's somewhere between Bonn and Koblenz, advance units of a tank division came upon a large bridge, the Ludendorfbrucke, still intact. A few of them managed to capture the bridge before the Germans caught on. Just at the last minute, the Germans managed to detonate a small charge fixed under the bridge, but it didn't do any damage. The Allies were soon in control of it, and thousands of soldiers, tanks, and armoured vehicles are moving across it right now."

"Terrific!" Kooiman shouted again.

"Right, that's what I thought, too, and I got swept along by the announcer's enthusiasm until I realized where I was.

"When the broadcast was over, the Ortskommandant began to recover a bit from his shock. He switched the set off and eyed me suspiciously, but I never moved a muscle. Then he went to great pains to assure me that the announcement was a 'lie' and 'propaganda.' You know, lies and propaganda are one and the same for the Germans because, of course, lies are what their propaganda is made of.

"Well, I nodded energetically, and in the end he actually believed his own explanation! But just to be sure, he tuned in to a German station that was just transmitting its version of the news. There was lots of talk about 'successful resistance,' 'defence flexibility,' 'strategic front concentration,' and a lot more of those transparent bits of jargon they use to snow listeners. But they never mentioned the bridge at Remagen! When I left fifteen minutes later, the Ortskommandant had some colour back in his cheeks. Still, I know he's scared because he realizes very well that the English broadcaster couldn't possibly have dreamed it all up, especially not with all the specific details he mentioned."

Greven stayed a while to savour the news. Kooiman fetched a large map of Europe showing the front lines. Most people had a map like that and reworked it constantly.

They checked to see exactly where Remagen was and speculated about what would happen and how long it would be before the end of the war. After the failure of the Battle of Arnhem, it was clear that the assault on Germany would not take place through the Netherlands. That would slow down the Dutch liberation, but it couldn't make too much difference. Once Germany fell, and it didn't matter how, the Dutch would be free too!

After an hour Greven left, and hope burned strongly in the hearts of the Kooiman couple.

For three days the German general staff censored all news about the Allied crossing of the Rhine at Remagen—not that that made much difference because Allied news reports were reaching all occupied territories despite German jamming devices. Even most of the Germans tuned in to them.

In the meantime, the German high command took measures to retake the bridge or destroy it. The best German troops were sent in to throw the Americans back, supported by what remained of the German Luftwaffe. But the Americans reinforced the bridgehead and began to spread out slowly on the east bank of the Rhine.

After three days the Germans could no longer black out news about Remagen. But they assured their listeners that soldiers of the glorious Reich would soon push the Americans back.

And, indeed, the Germans stepped up the pressure, and after ten days, the German Luftwaffe managed to destroy a section of the bridge. But by then the Americans had already built two new bridges. Slowly but surely the Allies consolidated their hold on the east bank.

Meanwhile, other American units were also trying to reach the Rhine. At the border between Belgium and Germany, they came upon the Siegfried line with its imposing bunkers and impressive underground tunnels. They had to take it section by section, but they finally secured it after heavy fighting. Further to the north, the English and Canadians had resumed their offensive toward the Rhine; they finally reached it on the tenth of March. They found that the Germans had blown up all the bridges across the river, but everybody knew that German resistance was virtually broken.

Back in the Netherlands it was time for the N.S.B.[10] to go underground. They had been so confident that this would never happen; they had always believed that although Berlin itself might be taken, the Allies would never be able to cross the Rhine. Now the Rhine had been breached, and it wouldn't be long before the Allies poured across the river at various other places. One look at the map left little doubt about that.

---

[10] the Dutch Nazi Party

CHAPTER TEN

NO TRESPASSING!

It happened one spring Saturday toward the end of March. Jan, Kris, and Jaap had gone out to look for lapwing eggs. It was a bit early in the season, but with this nice weather the boys found it impossible to stay indoors.

Jan and Kris hadn't been to school in three months, but they had managed to keep themselves occupied anyway. Nowadays they helped Kris' father with farm work. Jan also slept at the farm so that he could join them early in the morning. The days were long and the work hard, and the boys were always exhausted toward evening, but they enjoyed the work very much.

This morning, however, they'd been turned loose to amuse themselves. Kooiman judged that after five days of hard labour, they had earned some rest and recreation.

They had started out at six A.M. Mrs. Kooiman had given them some sandwiches and a thermos to take along.

They'd been out for three hours and had covered quite a bit of ground. At first the grass had been soaked with dew, but the sun had dried it out completely.

They had really enjoyed themselves even though they had found only two large eggs. They took a big pole along for vaulting across the ditches. Jaap, who had lived with the Kooimans for almost a year now, was quite skilled at vaulting ditches, but when it came to searching out eggs, he wasn't nearly as experienced as his friends. He was too easily fooled by the tricks lapwings used to foil any possible assailants.

It wasn't their fault that they hadn't been able to find more eggs. It was actually a little bit too early. The most important thing was that they were having fun. The warm spring sun and the balmy breeze were just what their spirits needed after the cold, depressing winter. They had enjoyed watching the lapwings, which always tried to mislead people from finding their eggs. They examined the ponds and the ditches to observe the miracle of new life awakening from winter sleep. It had been a lovely morning, much more like a day in May than in the chilly month of March!

By nine o'clock they were all getting tired and hungry.

Jan pointed to some bushes at the side of a footpath through the pastures. "Hey, let's sit down there and eat, shall we?"

"Right!" Jaap panted. He was tired; although no longer a weak, hungry little boy from the city, he still wasn't nearly as robust as his friends.

"All right, lets eat," Kris agreed. "We can't go farther anyway!"

He was right. A little farther ahead there was barbed wire all over the place. There was also a sign with a warning in German and Dutch that trespassers into the forbidden zone would pay with their lives.

There were now signs like that everywhere. Busy reinforcing their defenses, the Germans were building all kinds of antitank and antipersonnel obstacles. The operation was known as *Organisation Todt* and included an army of Dutch civilians forced to repair roads, dig ditches and trenches, and generally help the Germans prepare for coming invasions.

There were certain areas, like the one here, where only German soldiers were permitted.

The boys sat down on the warm side of the bushes, their faces to the spring sun. They took out the sandwiches and greedily chewed them.

Kris pulled out the two eggs he had found and inspected them. They were light green with dark brown spots.

"The Germans would pay a lot of good cash for eggs," he said. "But they're not getting these! I'd sooner throw them away!"

The others agreed. "The season's first lapwing eggs always used to be presented to the queen," Jaap informed them.

"Imagine these were the first to be laid, and we were sent up to the palace to present them to Queen Wilhelmina! Wouldn't that be neat!"

The others nodded enthusiastically. Jan remembered King David's three men who sneaked right through a Philistine siege to fetch King David some cool water from the cistern near Bethlehem. Talk about

66

heroes! Too bad they couldn't do that! Yes, it would be wonderful to take these eggs right to Queen Wilhelmina. Well, there was nothing wrong with daydreaming sometimes.

Kris stared at the area beyond the barbed wire. It was only a narrow stretch. The canal dike wasn't far from here, but the canal itself was hidden by the dike. There was a narrow road on top of the dike, just big enough for cars. That road went to a bridge across the canal, but nobody was allowed there anymore. Well, that didn't matter much because the road and the bridge were hardly used anyway. A few farmers thought the blockade was a nuisance. It was another indication that the Dutch were prisoners in their own country and that the Germans made the decisions.

Kris' attention was snagged by a couple of lapwings that darted around overhead and then disappeared into the high grass. He knew there had to be eggs there. Then he said, "I'm sure that there's a nest right next to the dike!"

"How do you know?" Jaap asked.

"Look at that bird. I've been watching him for some time. The nest is directly beneath him, I'm sure, and it wouldn't surprise me if there were eggs in it."

Jan sat up. He knew that Kris was probably right. He blinked a couple of times and then said, "You may well be right! Too bad we can't go there. There might be more nests next to the dike."

Kris stood up and looked in all directions. Nobody was around--not even on the dike.

"Let's risk it. Here, I'll take care of it. I should be back in five minutes, I hope with a few more eggs."

His friends hesitated. "It's dangerous," Jaap protested. "If the Germans see you, they'll shoot you."

"Ah, come on! There isn't a single German around!" Kris growled, knowing full well that Jaap was right.

Jan had also made up his mind. Checking the dike both ways, he said, "Let's risk it. It won't take but a minute!"

"Us? I'm going alone!" Kris exclaimed heatedly.

"Nothing doing! It's all for one and one for all! If all three of us look, it will take only half the time."

Kris protested meekly but finally agreed. "All right, then, but keep your eyes and ears open. Let's head straight for those bushes right next to the dike. The nest should be about thirty metres on this side of them."

They slid under the barbed wire carefully. Then they trotted off to the place Kris had pointed out, feeling a bit apprehensive, but also proud, because they were in clear violation of German regulations.

Kris was in front. Right about where he thought the nests should be, he stopped and said, "Let's start here." They started covering the ground, walking about a metre apart.

"Nothing here," said Jaap. But Jan pointed to the male lapwing that kept diving down on them, narrowly missing their heads.

"We must be getting close; otherwise he wouldn't be that nervous."

"There it is!" Jaap pointed to where the female was strutting around, her wings raised.

"Wrong again, Jaap! The female always struts away from the nest before she flies away. I'm sure the nest is closer to us."

Almost immediately Jaap saw that Kris was right. He spotted something nestled in a slight depression in the ground. He managed to stop just in time, a split second before he would have crunched three beautiful lapwing eggs underfoot.

The other two boys dashed toward him. They all bent over to admire their catch. The unhappy adult birds fluttered around screaming, but that didn't bother the boys.

Kris picked up the eggs and replaced them with a small potato he brought along to fool the birds. "Well, you beat me Jaap!" he said. "Congratulations!"

Jaap's cheeks blushed at this undeserved praise; he knew full well that he had almost made a mess of it. "I would never have found them if you hadn't shown me where to go," he admitted frankly.

From far away down the canal dike could be heard the sound of an engine. The brisk breeze muffled the sound, however, and the boys didn't notice a thing.

"Boy, we've got five eggs already," said Jan, satisfied. "That's worthwhile."

Kris nodded. "We'll have to remember where the nests were; next time around the catch will be even bigger."

Then his ear suddenly caught the engine sound; he wheeled around and his mouth dropped. "Germans! Let's get out of here!"

The military vehicle was approaching rapidly; it was already so close that the boys couldn't possibly made it back to the barbed wire in time.

Kris was the first to come to his senses. "Quick! Behind those bushes!" he yelled, pointing at some ragged underbrush growing along the base of the dike. It was their only chance, provided they hadn't already been spotted. They threw themselves down the side of the bank and lay flat behind the bushes, their hearts pounding wildly.

With bated breath they listened to the sound of the engine. There were still no leaves on the bushes, so their cover was minimal. Given the chance, they would have crawled under the dike. Kris felt responsible for the whole thing; what a dumb thing to do! He had risked not only his own life but also the lives of his friends. And why? Just for a couple of stupid eggs. It would be his fault if they were shot!

The engine noise became louder, until it was almost right on top of the boys. The roar and crunch of the wheels reverberated inside of the boys' heads.

Was it going to stop? No, it was going on. And now it was past.

For about half a minute, the boys didn't dare move. Then, one by one, they raised their heads and checked around.

Just then they heard the squeal of brakes as the truck came to a halt. The boys flung themselves down on the ground, their hearts suddenly pounding again. Surely they had been discovered!

They waited in silent panic, each of them raising a desperate cry to God for help. More minutes passed. Or were they hours? They lost all track of time, but one thing was beginning to sink in. There were no angry snarling voices and no guns being waved at them.

Kris finally worked up enough courage to turn his head. Out of the corner of his eye he peered at the top of the dike. He half expected to see a German with a gun trained on him, but there was nothing of the sort.

He lifted his head a little higher. Still nothing. He couldn't see the truck, but that didn't mean much. Even if it were only twenty metres away on the other side of the road, Kris wouldn't be able to spot it from here.

Suddenly they heard voices coming from somewhere on top of the dike close to where the truck must have stopped. So the Germans were there after all, but they hadn't spotted the three boys at the base of the dike.

The situation remained dangerous enough. They would have loved to try to run for safety, but they would probably have been seen before they got to the barbed wire. On the other hand, if they stayed here and one of the Germans happened to walk this way, they'd be spotted for sure.

If they only knew what those Germans were up to and how long they would stay there.

Kris made a decision; it was his fault, after all, that they were in this predicament. It was up to him to find a way out.

Not far away along the side of the dike there were some bushes and vines that grew right up to the top of the dike. Once there, he could scramble all the way up to see what the men were doing.

"You guys stay here. I'm going to take a look," he whispered to Jan and Jaap. Without waiting for their reply, he started to move sideways. Then, under cover of the bushes and vines, he worked his way upward.

Tensely, Jan and Jaap watched him clamber up the side of the bank. Only a couple of metres to go. Once he got to the edge, he slowly raised his head above the bank.

Anxiously, he peered across to the other side. His friends, meanwhile, were burning with curiosity. Then Kris turned halfway around, put his finger to his lips, and motioned them over. Immediately Jan and Jaap joined him. They lay down together on the steep embankment and lifted their heads just enough to see what was going on.

"Over there, to the left, by the bridge," Kris whispered urgently. A few soldiers were busy doing something or other. One of them was bringing a ladder over to the bridge, another was carrying a tool box in his hand, and one of his colleagues was unrolling some electrical wire. There was a fifth, a nom-com, who was supervising the whole thing.

The boys couldn't figure out what was going on. Probably some repairs to the bridge. But what was the electrical wire for?

They waited breathlessly for a while. One of the soldiers walked back to fetch a second ladder. The ends of the two ladders were dropped down into the canal until they came to rest on the bottom. Two men went down the ladder and began to fiddle around with the underside of the bridge. The three boys had no idea what they were doing.

High above them a German plane was circling in the sky. The boys suddenly realized how vulnerable they were. What would happen if they were spotted from above?

They waited until the airplane had disappeared, and then Kris whispered, "Let's get out of here; they're all preoccupied with the bridge now anyway. We can make a getaway, I think."

Kris was right, and yet the boys regretted not knowing what the Germans were up to. At any rate, they could get out of there alive.

Once more they looked back at the men still intent on their work. It didn't look as if they were going to be finished for a while, so this was the perfect opportunity to slip through the barbed wire back to safety.

CHAPTER ELEVEN

GERRIT GREVEN, A ONE-MAN ARMY

The boys quickly slid down the bank, picked themselves up when they got to the bottom, and rushed off toward the pasture.

It felt strange running away from German soldiers less than two hundred metres away. If one of them just happened to walk to the dike, he would see them immediately. In their imagination they could hear shots ringing out, but nothing of the sort happened. They reached the barbed wire without any trouble and breathed sighs of relief when they had slipped under it onto safer ground.

Despite the near disaster, Kris had managed to keep the five eggs safe. Their intrusion into the forbidden zone had been successful, and the boys felt immensely proud of themselves.

They didn't know what the Germans were up to, but they didn't really care.

"Let's go home," suggested Kris. "Five eggs is not bad at all for this time of year."

Feeling happy with their achievements, they started for home. After about twenty minutes, as they were coming to a sideroad, they saw Gerrit Greven on his bicycle.

When he reached the boys, he got down and started to chat with them. "Well boys, you've been out looking for crickets?"

"We've got something better than that!" replied Kris with pride. He untied the corners of his handkerchief and showed Greven the eggs. "Wow!" Greven whistled between his teeth when he saw the valuable eggs. "That's an excellent find!"

He paused for a moment and then said matter of factly, "I don't suppose you want to sell them? I'll give you a good price for them?"

Kris was about to agree, but then he checked himself. "What do you want them for?" he asked suspiciously.

"I'll take them to the German commander. He's crazy about them," Gerrit replied calmly.

Kris turned pale with rage. "No way the Germans are going to get these!" he replied angrily, quickly retying the corners of the handkerchief.

Greven's face turned cold and his eyes flashed momentarily. "You're right," he said bitingly. "Leave that dirty business to people like Gerrit Greven. The whole village believes him to be a traitor. But you ought to know better, Kris Kooiman, and so should you friends! You know very well what my job is. I have to deal with the Germans, and I don't like it any more than you do. Anyway, keep your precious eggs! I'll find something else."

He turned around sadly and reached for his bike.

The boys had all turned pale, and Kris was devastated. He seized Greven's sleeve and pleaded, "Greven, please, I didn't mean it that way. I wasn't thinking. Here, take the eggs and don't be angry with us anymore."

Greven laughed it off. "It's okay. I know you reacted without thinking—just name your price."

But Kris didn't want Greven's money. Greven was a hero. He didn't mind giving eggs to Greven, but under no circumstances would he sell them. So Greven, who sensed the boy's embarrassment, agreed. He took the eggs and asked matter-of-factly where they found them.

"Over there," replied Kris, pointing back to the canal. "The beauty of it is, we found a couple of them in the forbidden zone by the canal. We had quite an experience, I can tell you."

Greven's eyes widened. "You crazy guys! What's the idea of risking your lives for a couple of eggs? If the Germans had seen you, you'd be dead now. Come on, tell me what happened over there."

Kris already half regretted his confession. Greven was right; what they had done had been stupid! But Greven might as well know exactly what happened and how they were almost spotted by the German soldiers.

When Kris got to the part about the Germans working on the bridge, Greven's jaw muscles tightened and his eyelids narrowed. Two or three times he interrupted Kris to ask a couple of pertinent questions.

Apparently he wanted to know exactly what the boys had seen. So Kris told him everything he remembered about the affair. Jan and Jaap filled in a few more details Kris had forgotten.

When they had finished, Greven mused, "That's very interesting, boys. It's a good thing I know about it, but don't discuss it with anybody else."

"What do you suppose they were doing over there?" Jan asked, uncomprehending.

"Don't you get it?" Greven asked, a bit surprised. "They're rigging the bridge with explosives! That's what the electric wire was for. Should the Allies approach town from that direction, the Germans will blow up the bridge. Of course they don't want us to find out about that! If they had seen you boys there, you would have been done for. That's why I repeat: keep your mouths shut! If the Germans know that you saw them, they will kill you. Well, boys, thanks very much. I have to be going."

The dealer jumped on his bicycle and rode off while the boys continued their journey home. They had suddenly been relieved of their beautiful lapwing eggs, and they didn't have a penny to show for it. But they weren't at all unhappy. Let the Germans have the treats; it didn't matter at all as long as Greven got more vital information!

The boys didn't know exactly what Greven's job was, but they knew it was good. They didn't see why it was so important for him to know about the explosives that had been rigged to the bridge. Was he going to pass that information on to the Allies? What good would that do now?

They discussed it and came to no conclusions. In any event, they had enjoyed a fine morning and a most exciting adventure. And their discovery might prove useful to the Allies!

Their discussion with Greven made them feel that liberation wasn't very far off anymore. It might be only days before the first Allied tanks clattered through their village! They all secretly hoped they would be called upon to contribute significantly to the liberation. Their fantastic idea of helping the refugees arrest Hanekroot, Jonas Krom, and the mayor—and perhaps even the Ortskommandant—no longer seemed possible. The refugees were gone. But similar daydreams kept them preoccupied most of the time.

Several days later the bridge they had visited was reopened to traffic. All the signs were removed and it was no longer a forbidden zone.

Nothing seemed to have changed about the bridge. The Germans had done a good job of hiding the explosives. The only difference was that there was a sentry on patrol night and day. But sentries seemed to be almost everywhere.

Gerrit Greven rode past the bridge a couple of times and had casual chats with the sentry. But that didn't tell him very much. The dealer was beginning to work out a plan, a very dangerous one. He had to gather as much information as possible.

He got his information a week later. He paid a visit to the Ortskommandant's office. The man was in a meeting, so Greven had to wait a few minutes in one of the private offices. He took a quick look around to see if he could uncover something.

There was a large desk in the room. Greven sauntered over to it and opened a couple of drawers. One of them contained a map. Greven slid it out and quickly unfolded it. Inside was a drawing of the bridge showing exactly where the dynamite had been rigged. More important, Greven saw the type of explosive used. This was probably the sketch to show the soldiers how to do the job.

Greven had only about a minute or two to absorb the details. He heard footsteps coming and just managed to put the map back in place and close the drawer. This glimpse had been enough! Now he knew exactly what he wanted to know.

About fifteen minutes later, he left the mansion feeling very pleased with himself. He walked down the street, grinning from ear to ear. A couple of townspeople looked at him in disdain and mumbled among themselves. Gerrit Greven the Informer, they figured, had been to see his master again! But right now their mistaken hatred didn't bother him at all.

*   *   *

Night fell. The spring day had been light and sunny, and the evening was windy and chilly in contrast. The sentry stationed at the bridge across the canal had turned up his collar and was pacing back and forth to keep warm. Boring job, he grumbled to himself, to have a man watch an old bridge nobody ever used!

There was no moon, and the clouds scudding along the sky obscured the pale, dim light of the stars.

The darkness didn't bother the sentry much. It was more of a nuisance to Gerrit Greven. About a kilometre away from the bridge, he approached through some pastures. Sometimes he had to jump a ditch or climb over a gate. Other times he had to squirm his way through barbed wire. That isn't an easy task when you can't see what you are doing. Still, he was happy with the darkness; it gave him a fighting chance.

He bucked the wind. Under his left arm he clutched a tote bag. Finally he got to the canal dike where the going was easier even though the wind was blowing harder. Off to the side, he could hear the canal water lapping against the embankment stones.

Greven knew where he was going, and he also knew every inch of ground around here. Despite the pitch-black night, he had no trouble locating a rowboat moored to the embankment. He had a key for the padlock.

A minute later he was out in the middle of the canal punting toward the bridge. The slender craft bobbed on the unruly water, but that didn't bother Greven either. He knew a thing or two about boats and canals.

For the time being he was in no danger whatsoever, unless a German vehicle suddenly came to the canal dike. Even then chances were slim that they would spot him.

Greven punted steadily on toward the bridge. He could hardly see a thing, but he knew exactly the distance remaining.

About a hundred metres to go yet . . . Now only fifty metres . . . He pushed once more and them squatted down in the boat with the punting pole across his lap.

The rowboat slowly floated downstream. Now Greven could make out the bridge's silhouette. A few more seconds and he would be right under the bridge. Carefully he placed the punting pole on the bottom of the boat and then silently fastened the rope to the bridge.

The trick now was to give himself enough play so that the boat would drift to where the explosives were rigged.

Greven had memorized all the details of the drawing, but it was one thing to recall a few scratches on a piece of paper and quite another to locate the exact spot in the middle of the night while bobbing up and down in an unsteady rowboat.

He played out the rope slowly and noticed with satisfaction that the wind and the current were favourable. When he came to his target, he secured the rope, straightened up, and ran his hands along the steel girders of the bridge. He could just reach them.

He soon located a metal box that had been fastened to the bridge. He smiled happily; this had to be it!

Now for the tricky part. He needed a light to open the metal box and remove the explosives. But he knew that if the sentry spotted the light, all would be lost.

He reached into his tote bag and pulled out a flashlight and a piece of black cloth. He wrapped the cloth around the lens, leaving only a small part uncovered. Most of all, he had to avoid making a reflection in the water because that would give him away for sure.

Greven had deliberately inserted some batteries that were almost dead. When he flipped the switch on, the light was very weak. But it was enough. He spotted the latch on the cover of the box, slid it aside, and lifted the cover. Inside the box were a few sticks of plastic explosives and some wires.

He nodded; it all checked out. From his tote bag he took a piece of wood that had been painted to look like sticks of explosives.

With one hand he removed the charge, and with the other he clutched the steel girder. He had to be very careful not to leave telltale marks.

Next he inserted the piece of wood inside the box and fastened it onto the metal clamp.

He took one last look at his handiwork and closed the cover. He sighed quietly and deeply. As he was putting things back into the tote bag, he noticed that sweat was dripping down his face--not from exertion but from tension.

The worst was over. He untied the rope, picked up the punting pole, and shoved off. Every time he pulled the punting pole up for another shove, a few drops of water would drip, but fortunately that small noise was drowned out by the rushing of the wind. However, he didn't feel entirely safe until he was well away from the bridge.

It had been almost unbelievably simple. The sentry didn't notice a thing. Greven grinned gratefully.

In all likelihood the Germans would double-check the metal box to see if everything was still in place, but if they did, they probably wouldn't catch on because the wooden model looked very much like the original charge. They would not realize the truth unless they actually handled the explosives. But that wasn't likely.

Ever since he had heard from Kris and his friends what the Germans had done to the bridge, Greven had been intending to remove the explosives. He had never wanted to involve anybody else.

Would it make any difference to the outcome of the war? It would depend on the circumstances. In any case, if it was in the Germans' interest to rig the bridge, then it was in the Allies' interest to unrig it.

Greven punted on into the wind. It was even darker than it had been when he started out. But eventually he found his way back to where the rowboat belonged.

He moored the slender craft, replaced the chain and padlock, and clambered up the embankment. He walked along into the meadows. It was after curfew. Nobody was allowed out without a special permit. But way out here, in abandoned fields and windy weather, there was only a slight chance anyone would see him.

With a firm armlock on his tote bag, he disappeared into the darkness.

CHAPTER TWELVE

THE S.S. ARREST KOOIMAN

Farmer Kooiman came home slowly from his fields, bent over from a hard day's work.

True, he had Kris and Jan and sometimes Jaap to help him, but they were still children. Kooiman couldn't expect too much from them. He made up for it himself, usually spending from early morning until late at night in the fields.

As if that weren't enough, just recently he had been ordered to report to work at the *Organisation Todt*! The Germans kept needing men to dig trenches.

Kooiman had sneered at the N.S.B. mayor's orders. He had better things to do than help dig his own grave! He had torn the paper to shreds and tossed it into the fire.

Just this morning he had received a second notice; it was still in the inside pocket of his jacket. He pulled it out to reread it once more. It said, "An investigation has shown that you have not reported for work with the O.T. as ordered. It is imperative that you fulfil your obligations, and you are hereby summoned to present yourself forthwith upon receipt of this notice."

It was signed by the mayor himself.

Still Kooiman refused to go. He had sent a note to the mayor. Jaap had deposited the note in the mayor's mailbox. Kooiman had explained that he was much too busy with his farm work to conform to the mayor's request.

What he had written was true of course, and yet it was only half true. He was indeed much too busy for such nonsense, but more to the point, he was in no mood to work for the enemy!

His note probably wouldn't help anyway. Many of his fellow townsmen had been forced to work for the O.T., although they hated it.

Sooner or later they would come for him. But he wasn't about to give in now. How could he? The liberation was so near at hand. Giving in was against everything Kooiman believed in, and he was going to resist as long as possible.

If only he could be spared for a few more days. It was only a matter of weeks, maybe even days, before the Allies would get here. After Remagen the English had crossed the Rhine, and according to recent reports, they were planning an advance into the Netherlands from the east.

Kooiman wanted to stall the Germans as long as possible. If they came for him, he would take to the Wilds and stay there until the boys came to tell him that everything was all right.

It would be much safer if he went into hiding now, but that would be very costly to the farm later in the year. Food would be essential. So he stubbornly set his course. He was one solitary Dutch farmer thumbing his nose at the German war machine.

He didn't feel at all heroic, and he didn't for a moment deceive himself. Each day he faithfully asked God to protect his family and bring a speedy end to the war. But today he was particularly depressed. He had a feeling that something evil was around the corner. But he still refused to run.

He was soon back at the house. He walked into the kitchen where his wife was busy setting the table. Kris, Jaap, and Jan were also there.

Kooiman washed up, and then they all sat down for supper. As always, Kooiman prayed before the meal. And as usual they had mashed potatoes and buttermilk porridge. It was a very simple meal indeed, but for the millions of starving people in the western provinces, it would have been a feast.

They all ate their fill while discussing the events of the day. Jaap was the only one who had been to town. He had picked up some scraps of information, mostly rumours about lightning Allied thrusts through Germany and toward the Netherlands.

Kooiman perked up a bit. He hoped that his "one-man war" might not end before the big one did.

Supper finished, Kooiman took the Bible down from the cabinet and started to page through it. Just at that moment, they heard the roar of an engine outside. A large military vehicle bolted into the yard and stopped in front of the house. A squad of soldiers jumped out. A split second later, someone hammered on the front door of the farm house.

Kooiman's face had turned ashen. He felt like a rat in a trap. Though he had suspected the Germans might come sooner or later, he hadn't figured it would be this quick.

Plans for escape flashed through his mind, but a quick glance through the window told him that there was no way out because the soldiers had taken positions all around the house.One of them spotted him looking out and raised his rifle.

Just then the kitchen door flew open, and an officer, accompanied by two privates, charged into the house. They had come in through the unbolted back door.

"*Hande hoch!*[11]" the officer screamed.

Kooiman hesitated a moment, but when the officer thrust the barrel of his gun under his nose, the farmer thought better of it. The others, too, raised their hands.

Kooiman suddenly felt that there was something very wrong here. This visit concerned more than the O.T. job. The German faces betrayed implacable hatred. There was cold, killing rage in their eyes.

The officer ordered the family to back up against the wall, keeping their hands up. Then he walked up to the farmer, waved his gun in front of Kooiman's eyes, and screamed, "*Terrorist! Was hast du mit dem Poons gemacht?*[12]"

So that was it! Briefly, Kooiman thought he was going to faint. He started to drop his arms. A brutal blow to the jaw brought him back to his senses.

Fortunately, the officer didn't expect a reply right away.He began to

---

[11] Put your hands up!

[12] What have you done with Poons? (See The Grim Reaper, volume 3 of this series.)

rave and rant and threatened Kooiman with slow death at the hands of the Gestapo. The intimidation was intended to make Kooiman break down, but instead it gave him a few moments to recover from his shock.

If the Germans knew for certain that he had played a part in Poon's disappearance, he was lost. That much he knew. His only hope was that they were guessing. No matter what happened, he had to keep his mouth shut.

The officer had finished his tirade and paused just long enough to catch his breath. Then he ordered his subordinates to throw the "terrorist" into the truck.The soldiers shoved Kooiman roughly toward the door, leaving the rest of the family bewildered and dismayed.

The truck doors slammed shut, and the vehicle roared out of the yard.

Neither Mrs. Kooiman nor any of the youngsters had moved.Then Kris walked over to the window and watched the truck leaving. When he turned around, he saw his mother weeping quietly, both hands in front of her face.

The three boys stood still, feeling utterly lost. Tears were burning in their own eyes. They had all heard what the officer had said about Poons and realized that this was very serious.

Mrs. Kooiman quickly pulled herself together; she couldn't break down because she was now the only one responsible for the children and the farm.

Together they milked the cows and finished the minimal chores, weighed down by the fear that Mr. Kooiman would not escape a terrible doom.

Jan thought about his own father; he, too, had been arrested and had managed to escape. The same might happen with Mr. Kooiman. If Gerrit Greven heard what happened, he would do his best to find some way out.

Just before going to bed, they went through the whole incident again. Jan mentioned Gerrit Greven and thought he might be able to come up with a solution. But Mrs. Kooiman was less optimistic.

"It's possible they've got Gerrit too," she replied. "He was involved in the Poons affair, remember? In any event, he'll have to be extra careful now."

Before they retired they poured out all their fears to God. Then they finally went to bed, but it took a very long time before they were all asleep.

The next morning they got up early to help milk and feed the cows. With Kooiman gone, it took them a lot longer than usual.

Jaap stayed home from school that day to help the other two boys with the chores. There were lots of things to do. The three boys agreed that they would try to keep the farm going until Kooiman returned, hoping it would be soon.

That afternoon a man appeared whom they were longing to see: Gerrit Greven. The look on his face wasn't very encouraging. But at least he hadn't been picked up yet. Still, he didn't look very optimistic.

Once they had all gathered around the kitchen table, Greven began

84

to talk. He had been told the bad news that morning by a couple of German soldiers. It really jolted him, and he went directly to the Ortskommandant, presumably to see if he wanted some more supplies, and managed to get him to talk about Kooiman's arrest.

The Ortskommandant hadn't said very much, but Greven had learned that the arrest was indeed connected to the disappearance of this so-called Poons. There must have been a notice from Poons' investigation. The forged letter that had resulted in Poons' "transfer" must have turned up. It caused a furor.

Greven wasn't sure about the details, but he thought he had the general story. At this point he couldn't say whether there was any evidence against Kooiman.

Those were the things the dealer had to report. There were two other important facts he didn't dare to mention. The first was that the German officer had told him that Kooiman would be *erschossen*[13]. The second was that the commander's bearing and attitude toward him had been different. Greven was allowed to leave of his own free will and there had been no accusations against him, but little things told him that the Ortskommandant had begun to suspect him.

Greven thought it was better not to mention that. Things were bad enough for Mrs. Kooiman and the boys. He could tell from their faces that they hoped he would somehow add some good news. When Blankers was arrested, it was Greven who had found a way out. Blankers was rescued from the formidable Gestapo jail in the city. Kooiman was still in the village. Could nothing be done for him here?

Nobody spoke of that of course, but Greven could feel it.
And he knew full well the urgency of the matter! That terrible word *erschossen* was still ringing in his ears. But what could he do now? He was in great danger himself! He promised that he would do his best for Kooiman. But when he closed the door behind him, the only feeling left in his heart was deep despair . . .

---

[13] shot

CHAPTER THIRTEEN

GREVEN STICKS HIS NECK OUT

Cycling back, Greven concentrated on the current problem. The main difficulty was that he didn't have time to come up with a plan. These days the Germans didn't waste time with due process of law. They shot people down without provocation, without evidence, merely because of suspicion or suggestion. That's what probably would happen to Kooiman as well. Then again they might torture him to see what they could squeeze out of him.

Greven was pretty sure he knew where the farmer was locked up. Beside the Ortskommandant's villa was a second villa where the soldiers lived. Behind it the Germans had built a low-ceilinged, concrete building known as the bunker. The bunker housed various cells; Kooiman was undoubtedly in one of them.

The dealer went over the problem time and again. Finally he had an idea which he rejected almost immediately, but returned to it soon. In the garrison there might be a couple of soldiers who could be "bought." If Greven could manage to entice one of them, there might be a chance.

He reviewed the long list of names and faces he knew. Heinrich Schneider was probably the most likely to sell out to Greven. Schneider was an alcoholic.

Bribery might work, but Greven knew that it could just as easily fail. If Schneider, an untrustworthy drunk, reported Greven, he too would be killed. And even if he did succeed in rescuing Kooiman, they would both have to disappear fast. Greven would not be able to continue his work in the village. Well, that wasn't the worst thing. The Allies were banging on the doors anyway.

He tried to think of a better plan but failed. This was his only chance. If Schneider could slip him the key to the bunker and to Kooiman's cell, it would be easy enough to get Kooiman loose.

Greven rejected the idea of involving other members of the Resistance. That would only increase the risks. If necessary, Kooiman and he could hide in the marsh for a day or two; after that they could make their getaway.

That same night he began to work out his plan. Toward dusk he went to where the soldiers were garrisoned. The sentry didn't even question him; after all, Greven was a regular caller.
The Germans understood the art of scratching each other's backs and doing each other favours. Greven had taken along a suitcase filled with all kinds of goodies that were hard to get.

Having just finished supper, most of the soldiers were hanging around in the lounge. Only those scheduled for sentry duty later that night were asleep.

The soldiers gathered around Greven the moment he came in. Within a few minutes all his merchandise was gone.

Heinrich Schneider was there too. He was somewhat older than the rest—a brooding, sneaky man whose vocabulary consisted mainly of dirty words. He wanted to know if Greven had any schnapps. When Greven said no, he was visibly disappointed.

Though Greven had sold all his merchandise, he didn't leave right away. He chatted a bit with some of the men but couldn't get much out of them. In the meantime he kept a sharp eye on the man with whom he wanted to talk in private.

Some of the soldiers left to go into town. Presently, Schneider also left the lounge. A minute later, Greven snapped his suitcase shut and followed Schneider out the door.

Schneider was walking on the village square. Greven waited until the man had turned onto a quiet street and then cycled out after him.

There wasn't much time to lose; the dealer decided to get right to the point. He lowered his voice and said, "Schneider, I've got a special deal for you: a litre of the best cognac available--something you've never tasted before!"

The German's eyes lit up greedily. "*Wieviel?*"[14] he asked, supposing that Greven was after his money.

But Greven shook his head. "Won't cost you a penny! Just a favour."

Schneider was all ears; he wanted to know right away what he had to do for it.

This was it! Greven sensed he was risking everything, but under the circumstances, there was no other way.

Casually, as if it were something very trivial, he said, "It's about a good friend of mine, Farmer Kooiman. He was picked up yesterday and locked in the bunker. The poor guy hasn't done any harm, but he can't prove his innocence."

Greven halted. Schneider lowered the lids over his beady eyes.

"*Und?*" he demanded.

"Well, if you can arrange to have an innocent man escape, you've got yourself a bottle of the best cognac!"

The man's brain took a bit of time to work that out; then he shook his head vigorously. "*Unmoglich!*"[15]

But Greven wasn't about to let go that easily. Now that he'd gone this far, he might as well go all out. He assured the German that there was no danger involved. The good man Kooiman was pro-German, but a victim of a misunderstanding. Schneider wouldn't be involved at all. All he had to do was find out where Kooiman was locked up and make sure that the back door to the mansion was left unlocked for a short while one night. That was all. And nobody would ever connect him with Kooiman's escape!

Greven cranked up all his power of persuasion to convince Schneider. The German began to weaken. Before he agreed, however, he tried to demand two bottles of cognac. But Greven didn't have two.

At long last Schneider promised to consider Greven's proposal. He

---

[14] How much?

[15] Impossible!

told Greven to wait for him in the park the following afternoon. Schneider would meet him there. He warned Gerrit to bring the bottle of cognac because he would only go along with it if he were paid in advance.

Greven agreed. Then he got on his bicycle and went home. Deep down he didn't like this at all. He knew Schneider; the man was a bum. There was every chance that he would collect the bottle of cognac and then refuse to fulfil his part of the bargain. But it was a risk he had to take. Kooiman's life was at stake. And Greven was prepared to raise the stakes even higher by throwing in his own life.

*   *   *

There was a profusion of forget-me-nots in the park and lots of tender young grass. Birds were chirping and chattering in the trees. It sounded as if they were all debating where to build nests, but it was a bit early in the season for that.

The park belonged to the birds for the moment.

In less than an hour most of the neighbourhood mothers would come out with their baby buggies. They would sit down on park benches and enjoy the beauty of spring. Just now there was nobody using the park so soon after lunch. All the nearby streets were also deserted.

Deserted except for one man, a man on a bicycle–Gerrit Greven. He dismounted at the entrance to the park and walked in. He glanced around to see if anybody were watching him. But there was no one in the park.

Greven chose a park bench shielded by bushes on three sides. He leaned his bicycle against the backrest and sat down.

For a moment the birds stopped their chattering, waiting for the intruder to go away. They soon went back to their singing, play-fighting, and nest building. Despite a tightness in the pit of his stomach, Greven had to smile. Here he was, in the middle of the day, sitting in the park and looking up at the birds! Highly unusual. Would Schneider show up?

Greven's trained ear heard the sound of German hobnail boots. So he had come after all!

Schneider rounded the bushes and faced Greven. What an ugly face the man had! It suited him perfectly. Without any greeting, Schneider demanded, "*Wo ist die Flasche?*"[16]

"I've got it right here," replied Greven, showing the German the bottle in the inside pocket of his overcoat. "So you'll do it?"

The soldier nodded and leered at the bottle. Of course he was only interested in his cognac, but Greven wasn't about to give him the bottle without knowing more.

Schneider realized that; he sat down beside Greven and began to open up. Kooiman was in cell number five. There were no sentries watching the jail at night, only one at each door of the two mansions. The keys to the bunker were in a small room near the rear of the house. The back door to the house was locked at night, but Schneider agreed to unlock it at one o'clock in the morning and then lock it again soon after. Greven would have exactly half an hour to open Kooiman's cell and return the keys to the house. For the rest, Schneider didn't want to be involved.

Greven listened intently. He took in all the details but also watched Schneider very carefully, trying to read between the lines. Was the man going to double-cross him? Greven couldn't be sure. But one thing he was sure of, he would go tonight.

Schneider had done his part and held out his hand. Greven slipped the bottle to him, and the German quickly hid it under his tunic and got up and left.

Greven waited a few moments. Then he too got up and went off in the opposite direction.

Once home, he worked his plan out carefully. First he would have to get to the mansion without being seen. That was no problem. Next, he would somehow have to cross the property to the rear without the sentry's seeing him. But he would manage that too. He didn't expect any problems on either count.

Then he would have to go inside the house for the keys. That's where Schneider came in. Would that drunken no-good double-cross him?

---

[16] Where is the bottle?

He might guzzle the whole bottle of cognac that night and "forget" about unlocking the door.

That was the major risk.

The rest was easy. Greven would take the keys to the bunker, first open the outside door, and then open cell number five.
Kooiman would probably be asleep already, so he would have to quickly wake him up and tell him what was going on.

Then he would have to get the two of them out of town and head for the Wilds. They would have to hide in the hunting shack until they could arrange to be shipped elsewhere.

The Ortskommandant would be livid. He would probably be able to figure out what had happened, but he'd have to get up pretty early in the morning to catch them! Greven sat down for supper, but he didn't feel much like eating. Time crawled. Shortly after midnight he put on his long overcoat, jammed a wide-brimmed hat on his head, and shoved a flashlight into his pocket.

That was all he needed; no need to take a weapon. He would need brains, not weapons, for this little caper.

He checked his watch; it was 12:30 A.M.–time to leave. Quietly he slipped out through the back door.

CHAPTER FOURTEEN

DOUBLE-CROSSED!

Greven lived on the edge of town. His destination wasn't far, but the dealer decided not to take the most direct way. Under no circumstances did he want to be seen. He took to the alleys where he didn't expect to find any Germans or policemen at this time of night. So a full half hour lapsed before he finally got to his destination.

He crossed through a number of gardens to approach the mansion from the rear. That meant getting past a hedge and three rows of barbed wire. Barbed wire wouldn't stop Greven. He had already checked this place out and discovered he didn't even need wire cutters.

The sky was completely overcast, and that suited him fine too. The darkness didn't bother him one bit. He knew exactly where everything was.

He came upon the path through the garden and followed it to the rear of the two mansions.

What time was it now? He figured it must be at least one o'clock. Still, it was safer to wait a bit. He sat down on the ground with all his senses tuned. He had to be absolutely quiet because there were no other noises in the square to cover his sounds. Everything around seemed dead. So far as he could tell there were no lights burning in the mansion, but he knew that there were three sentries nearby. Any noise at all, and they would sound the alert.

Greven still had doubts about Schneider. The three sentries posed no danger at all, but what scared him was that despicable Heinrich Schneider. Could he trust him? Well, it was too late for that now. He had to go on. Kooiman's life depended on it!

It must be after one o'clock now, he reflected. He had to make his move, or he would run out of time. He got up, feeling chilled to the bone from the cold night air.

He carefully made his way down the path toward the house. By now his eyes were used to the darkness. That dark hulk off to his left was the bunker. Only a few more metres and he would be at the back entrance to the mansion.

With all his nerves and muscles coiled, he tiptoed to the back door and ran his fingers along the wall.

To his immense relief and surprise, Greven found that the door was unlocked. So Schneider had kept his word after all!

Slowly he pushed the door open, happy that the hinges didn't creak. He opened it just far enough to slip through and then closed it behind him. For about a minute he stood there with his back against the door while he tried to figure out where to go. It was even darker here than it was outside! He feared a trap.

Everything remained quiet, and gradually he became convinced that there was nobody else in the hall. He edged his way to the next door.

He found the next door in the dark successfully. Sure enough, when he turned the doorknob he found that this door was unlocked also.

Now he needed his flashlight. For only a second or two he shone the beam through the room, but it was enough to reveal a small cabinet built into the wall. Its door was closed and the key was in the lock.

When he turned the key, the lock clicked noisily. It sounded like a pistol shot to Greven. He was convinced he had awakened everybody in the building and that they would soon come swooping down on him. He fought down the panicky urge to flee before an alert was sounded.

After a few seconds, he had recovered; he knew that the click couldn't possibly have wakened anybody. But suppose somebody hadn't been sleeping?

"Come on," he scolded himself, "this is no time to waver. "Everything stayed quiet as time was running out. He opened the door to the cabinet and briefly shone his flashlight inside.

There were various keys inside. The large one was the one to the bunker's main door. There were several smaller keys with numbered tags on them. He quickly removed the large key and the key tagged number five. He thought the other cells weren't in use just now so he wouldn't open them.

So far so good; he optimistically retraced his steps, closed the back door, and then glided toward the bunker.

He couldn't use his flashlight here, but he knew exactly where the outside door was. Now where was the keyhole? Suddenly, he felt unaccountably nervous. Was there something moving over there by the bushes? Must be his imagination. He needed to keep calm. The door readily opened, and Greven sneaked inside, heading down the corridor toward cell number five.

Then, suddenly, a blinding light lit up the entire hallway! Greven, with the keys dangling from his hand, froze on the spot in terror. A large flashlight was aimed at him.

The voice of the German Ortscommandant sneered at him. Would he really like to see the inside of a cell? Well, the man laughed sarcastically, he would get his chance! But first Greven was told to drop the keys on the floor and raise his hands.

Greven didn't react right away; his brain was working feverishly at an escape plan. Then a shot rang out, and a bullet whined past his ear.

"*Stehen bleiben und Hande hoch!*"[17] He couldn't ignore that, so he obeyed.

He had no chance to escape. The Ortskommandant was accompanied by three German soldiers, all armed with pistols. They must have been lying in wait for him beside the bunker.

One of them was Heinrich Schneider with a smug grin on his face. Greven had an urge to grab him by the throat, but he knew that would be stupid. They seized Greven roughly, and the soldiers emptied his pockets. They also punched him in the face several times. His nose started to bleed. They sneered at him for having been so stupid as to walk into an obvious trap like that.

Greven wisely remained silent; it was the only defense he had. He knew about the cruel methods the Germans used. First they tried to break their victim with physical and verbal abuse. At some point the cruelty would change to a show of friendliness and even compassion to get the tormented victim to break down and spill his secrets. But they wouldn't get him that way!

After they had gone through his pockets, one of the soldiers opened the door to cell number five and kicked him inside. Then the door was slammed shut and the key turned in the lock.

After the blinding light of the flashlight, the darkness was heavy and oppressive. Then he heard a familiar voice say, "Gerrit, is that you?" Kooiman had been startled out of his sleep by the gunshot and had picked up scraps of the conversation.

Kooiman's voice was a real comfort in this tragedy.

---

[17] Stay where you are and put your hands up!

Greven felt his way across to the cot, sat down, and told his friend what had happened.

Kooiman was both appalled and moved with pity. When he had heard Greven's story, he was moved to tears and put his arm around his companion. "I want to thank you, Gerrit! You've put your life on the line for me!" But Greven shook it off; he was furious with himself for having allowed himself to be taken in by that good-for-nothing Heinrich Schneider! He realized very well that he would probably never get revenge. There were only two things he could look forward to: painful interrogations and, after that, a bullet through the head.

For years he had prepared himself for this, ever since the day he had enlisted with the Resistance out of sheer hatred for the Nazis. He had always managed to survive, though he had had his close calls. And now, just as liberation was at hand, he had been double-crossed by a scoundrel like Heinrich Schneider. He might die just hours before the English and Canadians arrived on the scene. Needless to say, neither of the men slept much that night. They talked until the early hours of the morning.

Kooiman had already been through a couple of terrible days. He had been interrogated twice with the customary beatings. When the first light of dawn fell through the barred window high above them, Greven could see the welts, cuts, and bruises on the farmer's face.

So far Kooiman had been given the strength to bear it. "Given the strength," that's how he put it, and Greven realized immediately that Kooiman was completely serious about that. Kooiman had been given the kind of strength that Greven lacked: the strength of his Christian conviction.

CHAPTER FIFTEEN

THE SHADOW OF DEATH

The news of Greven's arrest spread through town like a brush fire. The German soldiers discussed it openly, and within hours everybody knew about it.

Most of the villagers didn't know what to think. They had always considered Gerrit Greven a profiteer and an ally of the hated Germans. Had they been wrong about him after all? Some people suspected that there was more to it than they knew. Mrs. Kooiman had probably promised Greven a large reward if he succeeded in getting her husband free. Characters like that would do anything for money.

These were some of the rumours making the rounds, but very few people knew anything close to the truth. Those who knew about Greven's double role in the community wisely kept their mouths shut. Any slip of the tongue would only make matters worse for Gerrit and Kooiman. And things were bad enough!

A few curious souls even went to the Kooiman farm to express their sympathy and at the same time try to find out why Kooiman had been arrested in the first place and how Greven had gotten into the picture. But Mrs. Kooiman kept silent and got rid of the inquisitive gossips as fast as she could. They were a little bit indignant with her that she was so inhospitable.

She could talk about it only with the three boys. After all, they knew exactly what had happened. But they, too, were sunk in deep despair, although they did their best not to show it.

For Jaap, school was over now also. The school building had been taken over by the Wehrmacht. The whole village was in a state of seige.

The four of them kept the farm going as best they could. It was hard work, and they couldn't do everything.

Mrs. Kooiman was not only grieving about her husband but she also blamed herself for Gerrit Greven's arrest. It was to help and comfort her that Greven had promised to do something on behalf of her husband. Since Kooiman was gone now, she was the one who read from the Bible and led in prayer at the table, never ceasing to ask God to bring deliverance for the two men. The boys prayed for that on their own also, including Jaap, who had learned to pray during his stay on the farm.

Despite the fact that the three boys were busy with farm work, they were almost constantly preoccupied by plans to rescue the two prisoners.

They knew, of course, that if Gerrit Greven couldn't succeed, they wouldn't stand a chance. But that didn't prevent them from thinking and talking about it. They always ended with some hare-brained scheme that was totally impractical and far too dangerous.

Whenever they were in town, they would loiter around the two mansions, hoping to catch a glimpse of Mr. Kooiman and Mr. Greven. But all they ever got to see was a corner of the bunker.

There was really only one hope: that liberation would come before the men were executed. Could it? They knew that prisoners were taken out to the country and shot without due process of law. And the boys were sure that was what would happen to these two prisoners if the Allies got anywhere near the town. So they were faced with a real dilemma: while hoping fervently for the long-awaited liberation, they also feared what it might mean.

The Allied offensive was in high gear. Fanning out their armoured divisions once they crossed the Rhine, the Americans had surrounded the entire industrial area of the Ruhr. Large parts of the Netherlands east of the IJssel River had already been liberated, and the Allies were just now moving into the northern provinces.

Just to the south of the Rhine, the Allied advance had been frustrated by poor road conditions, preventing the Allies from crossing the Rhine at Arnhem and moving into the western provinces. Indeed, liberation could come any day now, but the people in the village and in the rest of the central and western provinces still had to wait and suffer increasing German terrorism.

Kooiman and Greven weren't allowed the pleasure of staying in the same cell. On the morning following Greven's arrest, the German Ortskommandant realized it was a mistake to keep them together.

He called Greven in for questioning that very morning, but he had had enough time to think through his story and handled himself beautifully.

He admitted that trying to free Kooiman had been a mistake, but he had done it with the best of intentions. Kooiman was an old acquaintance of his after all. The farmer had often provided him with lots of useful items to sell. Greven was sure that the accusation against Kooiman was based on a misunderstanding. He had wanted to discuss things with Kooiman in confidence, just to try to clear the whole thing up. True, it would have been better to get clearance from the Ortskommandant, but he hadn't wanted to involve anyone. Looking back, he was sorry about that, of course.

It was a fantastic yarn, but the dealer sounded so convincing that he almost believed it himself.

The German face, however, remained cold and hostile. In the end he told Greven it was all nonsense.

But Greven persisted, pleading his case eloquently, like a good lawyer. Sometimes he had the feeling that he was making headway. But he was also afraid that the Ortskommandant knew or suspected something about his role in the Resistance. In the end he was brought back to the bunker and locked up in a cell next to Kooiman.

He was dead tired; the emotional drain of the questioning, the lack of sleep, the disaster of the night before, and the loneliness were almost too much for him. He dropped despondently to the iron cot.

Suddenly he heard a soft ticking. It seemed to come from a metal pipe, a hot water heating pipe that ran horizontally along the back wall.

Greven jumped up, walked up to the pipe, and ticked out a reply.

Then he heard Kooiman saying, "Is that you Gerrit?"

Greven lowered his head to where the pipe disappeared through the wall. It was surprisingly easy to carry on a discussion with the occupant of the next cell, using the pipe as a sound conductor. He told Kooiman what had happened to him and the story he had given. That would be useful if Kooiman himself were questioned again. The Germans could be expected to play the accounts of the two witnesses off against each other.

The hot water pipe connection proved to be very useful. The next morning Kooiman was called in for questioning. Again he was beaten and abused, but again he revealed no secrets. Once he was back in his cell, he reported to Greven, but he did not mention the beatings.

That afternoon Greven was called in again. On the German's desk were some of Greven's personal possessions; apparently they had already searched his house.

That didn't bother Greven much. The articles they weren't supposed to find were hidden elsewhere anyway. But it showed him that the Ortskommandant was highly suspicious.

The Ortskommandant went through the things they had picked up at his house, including some gear for developing film. Greven calmly admitted that they were his and gave an innocent explanation. The German was clearly annoyed that he couldn't seem to upset Greven. Apparently the officer didn't quite know what to think of him.

Again he was sent back; once again he had passed a major test. But Greven felt impending doom. Sooner or later they had to stumble onto something he wouldn't be able to explain.

Two days passed and the two prisoners had many talks. During these days Kooiman also pointed Greven quietly to the only comfort in life and death.

The dealer had never been a religious man, but he became impressed by Kooiman's earnest words and the peace and strength that the farmer received from his faith. Deep down in his heart, he envied Kooiman for his peace of mind.

It seemed clear to him that this imprisonment would end in death. The Germans hadn't believed his story and kept digging and rooting around. They would eventually find something to incriminate both him and Kooiman.

That didn't take long. On the third day after his capture, he was called in for questioning again. This time they used handcuffs on him. That was a bad omen, although it could mean that they were simply trying to frighten him.

He acted calm, but inside he was torn apart. With the German Ortskommandant was an S.S. officer whose cold blue-grey eyes stared at the dealer in disdain.

Greven was made to stand as the S.S. man took a paper from the desk and began to read.

Before he had finished a couple of lines, Greven felt as if his universe was collapsing. It was a confession written by the German who used to work in the Ortskommandant's office who had given Greven all kinds of highly confidential information. Apparently the man had made a slip, had been arrested, and had made a full confession. Among other things, he confessed to typing up a letter for Greven announcing Poon's transfer elsewhere.

When he finished reading, the S.S. officer said coldly, "This traitor is to be shot today. The same goes for you. You have one chance. Give us the names of your associates and everybody in the village who's connected with the Resistance. If you do, we'll temper justice with mercy."

He halted in hopes of cooperation. But by this time Greven had already recovered from the blow and quietly replied, "I have nothing to say. That so-called confession is just a fake."

Both Germans leaped from behind the desk. The Ortskommandant yelled at Greven, and the S.S. officer started to beat him viciously.

Gerrit didn't say a word. At long last he was returned to his cell, his face covered with blood, his lips swollen, and some of his teeth knocked loose.

Although his silence might save the lives of others, he and Kooiman were doomed. The die was cast.

CHAPTER SIXTEEN

BREAKTHROUGH!

One day Blankers was alone out in the open field. He had been on the farm for a couple of weeks with his friend Cor. They couldn't have found a better place. But lately restlessness was eating at Blankers. News and rumours about the Allied advance abounded, but not a Canadian soldier had appeared yet.

The carpenter told himself to be patient. He had been waiting for five years. A few days more or less didn't matter.

That's how he tried to soothe his rising impatience, but it didn't help. At night he could hardly sleep because of homesickness. If only he could do something to contribute to the liberation. But there were no more assignments. Willem seemed to have forgotten about Cor and him.

The car was still hidden in the barn. Cor's arm mended well, and the two refugees enjoyed helping the farmer with his chores. But they missed Resistance work.

Today was one of Blankers' bad days. Everything was too much for him. He had walked way out into the field without saying anything. For hours he had been strolling across the fields, deep in thought, trying to tell himself that the war would soon be over. Now he was on the way back, tired and hungry. The long cross-country walk had done him some good. He had managed to come to peace with himself. He had also prayed that God would grant him patience and would take care of all who were dear to him.

When the farm was just over the next hill, he sped up a bit. It was time for lunch and he was famished.

Just as he crested the hill, he saw Cor running toward him, waving his arms. Suddenly worried, Blankers wondered what could be the matter.

When Cor got within earshot, he shouted, "They're across!"

"Who? Across what?" asked Blankers.

"The Allies, across the IJssel River! They're coming in from the east. Their tanks have already made it to Arnhem. There's heavy fighting there!"

Arnhem! Blankers felt a jolt. There were so many sad memories connected with that city. So the time had come!

Cor had a lot to tell. The Germans had expected the Allies to attempt a crossing of the lower Rhine west of Arnhem. For some time English pioneers had been building a bridge secretly in Nijmegen. Instead of moving it north to the lower Rhine, they took it across the main Rhine east of Nijmegen and from there north to the IJssel River. Without the Germans even knowing about it, the Allies crossed the IJssel, thus making a crossing of the lower Rhine unnecessary. The Germans were taken by complete surprise when tanks rolled into the Arnhem suburbs!

Cor had more news; the IJssel River had also been crossed some distance to the north, and liberation of the western provinces was in full swing.

Now both Blankers and Cor were deeply excited. Cor slapped the carpenter on the shoulder and said, "You know what we should do? We should go out to meet them and volunteer as guides. I know all the roads and trails in this country like the back of my hand. When we get there, we'll ask them to give us some tanks and armoured cars, and we'll go and liberate your town!"

Cor sounded drunk; what he was suggesting was madness. Blankers hesitated at first, but he was soon carried away by the excitement of the thing. Once they calmed down a bit, they started back for the farm, talking things over as they went.

They had the van and a little bit of gasoline too, maybe even enough to reach the Allied lines. Anyway it would take them as close as they needed to go.

True, they might run into the Germans on the way. But they still had all kinds of official-looking papers, and Cor could talk his way out of anything.

They sensed that the risks were much greater than they were willing to admit. There was still a war going on. Any civilian caught between the lines was risking his life. But they had already experienced much danger. Doing something, anything, seemed better than just sitting here. This might be their big chance.

They had already made their decision when they got back to the farmhouse. After lunch they would take the van in search of the Allied armies. The farmer advised against it, but by now there was no stopping them.

Right after lunch they fetched the van out of the barn. There wasn't as much gasoline as they had hoped, but they would see how far they could get. They left half an hour later.

Cor drove and Blankers sat beside him. If they were stopped, they would pretend to be officials for Food Administration. Cor already had his story ready, and they should be able to make it.

For a while the two adventurers refused to be bothered by anything. It was a gorgeous sunny day with a brisk wind and a clear blue sky. Excitement had gotten hold of them, and they forgot about caution for a change.

They stuck to deserted back roads as much as possible and made pretty good time. But at an intersection they suddenly were stopped by three German sentries who told them to go back.

Cor started to tell his story and tried to show the men his papers, but the non-com in charge wasn't at all impressed. Nobody was allowed to go in that direction, he explained. *"Befehl ist Befehl."*[18] And that was the end of it.

Cor turned the car around, planning to make a detour and try again elsewhere.

Again they were stopped by sentries. Cor tried to impress the soldiers with a sense of urgency, but one of the Germans reached for his rifle and threatened to shoot the insolent Dutchman through the head. They turned around and started back quickly because it was beginning to look as if the soldiers wanted to confiscate the van.

Under the cover of some trees, they stopped to review their plans. Apparently all the roads going east were being watched. They could

---

[18] a rule is a rule.

easily cross the German lines on foot, but in order to reach the Allied lines, they would need a car.

Cor lapsed deep into thought. Finally he said, "I think I know a solution. Anyway, it's our only chance."

He started the engine and found a road that went north. It wasn't clear to Blankers what Cor was up to, and he didn't bother asking. Cor knew this area much better than he.

They soon came to hilly terrain, and Cor turned off onto a side road. Then they drove into some woods. This road wasn't really a road at all, just a winding path! Cars weren't even allowed here. There were tree roots and potholes everywhere. Fortunately the trail was just wide enough for the van. Cor pulled up just short of the main highway that cut through the woods. They had to cross it; this was a critical spot.

They got out and made their way to the roadside. There wasn't a single German around. They walked back to the van and were just about to cross the highway when Cor heard a roar from the left. He backed up quickly. Seconds later a long column of German military vehicles sped past less than ten metres away. The two men could easily see the tired, dejected look on the German soldiers' faces. If any one of them had glanced to the side, he would have spotted the van immediately. But either nobody saw them or nobody cared even if they did.

Some field artillery brought up the rear of the column. After they had passed, everything became quiet once again.

"Now it's our turn," Cor said simply. They crossed the highway without a hitch and were soon back on the path through the woods, heading east. About fifteen minutes later they emerged from the woods, and Cor stopped once again to size up the situation. Ahead of them lay more hills covered with dense underbrush. The path narrowed to a sandy trail hardly suitable for their van.

They climbed a relatively high hill to their left. From its crest, they could see far to the east and south.

The sun had gone down behind them, but the pastel colours of the evening sky still lit up the field. The wind had died down. In the distance were the steeples of a city and a few smaller villages.

Suddenly their reverie was broken by heavy thuds, followed by a rumbling echo. Briefly the eastern sky lit up and then darkened again.

Artillery! Far off in the distance, field batteries had opened fire, signalling the coming of the Allies.

The two men quickly glanced at each other and then ran down the hill toward the van.

The van struggled sluggishly down the sandy trail. Cor checked his fuel gauge and saw that there was practically no gas left.

They managed to go a couple more kilometres before the engine coughed a few times and then went dead.

Cor looked around; off to his left was a trail that led down into a gravel pit.

"Let's leave the van down there," he suggested. "Nobody will notice it there, and they won't be able to move it anyway. We may be able to come back in a couple of days to pick it up."

Blankers agreed that this was the best solution. He went to the back of the van and pushed while Cor steered. Going downhill was easy, and once they got to the bottom of the gravel pit, the van was pretty well out of sight. Cor took the keys out of the ignition and put them into his pocket. They would have to travel on foot now.

It was getting dark, which was both good and bad for them. They wouldn't be as easily detected in the dark, but the darkness increased their chances of bumping into a German patrol. They would never be able to explain what they were doing between enemy lines. In all likelihood they'd be shot on the spot.

So they had to be on guard. They whispered only when necessary and carefully checked out every bend in the trail.

There was no more artillery fire, but they heard a strange noise in the distance that they couldn't identify.

Soon they emerged from the overgrown, sandy hills and found themselves on the edge of some open fields and pastureland. From here on there wouldn't be much cover, but by now it was almost completely dark anyway.

They walked for about forty-five minutes and began to approach a rather large town. They could distinguish the steeples of some churches and the rooftops of row housing. The strange sound grew louder. It seemed to be coming from this town. It was a roar of human voices mixed by all kinds of other sounds, but neither Cor nor Blankers had a clue what it was all about.

Were the Germans doing something dreadful? Or had the town been liberated? They didn't know and they realized that much was depending on the town's liberation. Any moment now they could expect to run into sentries.

Suddenly they stood stock still. The babble of voices was overcome by the sound of trumpets, which began to play a melody: the *Wilhelmus!*[19] The two men listened as they heard hundreds of people join in singing. They could easily understand the words. Blankers wanted to sing along, but he couldn't. His throat was constricting, and tears coursed down his face. All the suffering and yearning of the past five years, those terrible, painful years, and all the fearful memories of persecution and death seemed to fall away in this moment of overwhelming happiness. When after the first stanza the people started singing the sixth, Blankers managed to join in softly:

> *Mijn Schild en de Betrouwen*
> *Zijt Gij, o God, mijn Heer*[20]

Cor stood straight beside him in silence. His right hand came up in a military salute as befits a soldier listening to the national anthem on the day of liberation.

As the last sounds of the melody died away, the two friends began to run toward the town, certain now that liberation had come.

Just before they got there, however, they bumped into two Canadian sentries armed with submachine guns.

Cor spoke English fairly fluently; he explained that they had crossed over from the occupied territory and had important information.

---

[19] the Dutch national anthem

[20] My Shield and a Reliance, art Thou, O God, my Lord

The sentries were not convinced, and in the end one of them accompanied the two to battalion headquarters. He told the two men to walk in front of him, and he kept his submachine gun aimed at their backs. Apparently he wasn't taking any chances.

Cor and Blankers didn't mind at all. They were busy trying to take in everything they saw around them. There were tanks, armoured cars, jeeps, and other war materials spread throughout the whole town. Flags waved from nearly every upper story window. Canadian soldiers were walking around, talking with the villagers. Most of the people were just leaving the village square. That's where the festivities had taken place, and excited people were spreading out through the streets, still having the time of their lives. With the pressure and fear gone, people were free to laugh and joke for the first time in five years. Dozens of young people were running around yelling, and some older people were just as wild with happiness. What a celebration it was!

Amid the happy chaos, the Canadian soldier escorted Blankers and Cor to the hotel that had been taken over by the battalion staff.

Minutes later they found themselves in a large room with three Canadian officers and a civilian. The sentry gave a brief explanation and then left.

The oldest of the three officers, probably the commander, approached Cor and Blankers and asked them what they were doing there.

Cor retold his story. He explained that they were members of the Resistance who had escaped from the occupied territory. He told him that he knew this area inside out and knew a perfect place to slip in behind enemy lines. He told the officer they would be glad to act as guides.

The man waited patiently until Cor had finished. His dark brown eyes seemed to want to pierce right into the two men to see if they were speaking the truth. Cor couldn't tell from his face whether he believed him or not.

When Cor had finished, the commander exchanged a few whispers with the civilian. The civilian then said to Cor in Dutch, "So, you're members of the Resistance. Tell me more about it. Which group do you belong to? Give me some names and some details."

Briefly, Cor struggled with himself. For years he had trained himself to keep secrets, and now he was being asked to give names of his Resistance friends! Quickly he told himself that different rules applied now. He wasn't being questioned by the enemy, but by the Allies. This was no longer occupied territory, and there was no reason why he shouldn't open up.

The civilian asked some helpful questions that showed he knew all about the Resistance. When Cor mention Willem, a smile appeared on the man's face.

"I know Willem very well," he said. That proved to be decisive. The civilian explained that he had once been mayor here but had been removed by the Germans. From his questions and from the way he fielded Cor's answers, it was pretty clear the man himself had participated in the work of the Resistance. He was soon convinced that Cor and Blankers were reliable and assured the Canadian officers of that also.

Suddenly the ranking officer became much more agreeable. He invited Cor and Blankers over to a table that had an area map on it. One of the officers marked in details the German defenses, based on what Cor and Blankers told him. He also marked out a route that would take them through German lines without any difficulty.

Finally the commanding officer said he wanted to think about it. At first glance it seemed there were too many risks involved. Even if they were to break through enemy lines, they would have to do so with a relatively small force. Once inside enemy territory, they might easily be cut off and surrounded by Germans. On the other hand, if the manoeuvre were successful, the Germans might panic in a disorderly retreat. That could save both time and human lives.

He promised to get back to them the next morning to tell them whether he could use their services. They could stay overnight in the hotel.

The officer left because he had much more to do. Cor and Blankers were taken to another room where they were served a meal of white bread, cheese omelettes, cakes, and other such treats they hadn't tasted in years.

Feeling quite content, they were led to an upstairs bedroom with two single beds. Before turning in, however, they stood on the balcony for a while and listened to the festivities that would no doubt go on till far into the night. There seemed to be no end to the hubbub. The longer it lasted, the more boisterous the remaining people seemed to become.

"Now they're all fanatic patriots, of course, but you should have seen most of them when the Germans were here. Too frightened to lift a finger to help anybody. And that's how it was all over."

There was deep bitterness in Cor's voice. Blankers could well understand. His companion was reflecting on the difficult years that lay behind. He was thinking of so many of his friends who had died for a nearly impossible cause. It was true that thousands of Dutch people had been too scared to do anything for the cause. Nevertheless, Blankers couldn't share Cor's bitter feelings, and he told him that also. This had been a day for happiness and gratitude. God had done great things for a people who had departed from His ways in many things and who had seemed to no longer have any future.

Cor listened to Blankers and in the end nodded. He too was thankful for this deliverance.

When they finally lay down they were dead tired both from the journey and from the emotions of the day. Blankers' head was almost spinning. Well, he wasn't going to try to figure it all out. Not today anyway. Smiling, he surrendered his overworked body to a restful sleep.

CHAPTER SEVENTEEN

THE FIRST DAY OF PEACE

That day Kooiman and Greven were left alone for a change. They spent most of the day talking with each other along the hot water pipe. Greven informed Kooiman about the soldier's confession. Both knew their time had run out. They hoped only that they wouldn't have to suffer any more painful interrogations and Gestapo torture. It would be terrible if they broke under torment and betrayed others. They would rather die quickly!

But the prospect of dying, especially just before the liberation, was almost too much for Gerrit Greven. He had no dependents, but he dearly loved life. Still, he reflected, it must be a lot harder for Kooiman to leave a family behind.

Greven was astonished to see, however, that the farmer accepted it rather calmly. It was his faith in Christ that enabled Kooiman to look straight at the facts and yet be comforted. Kooiman trusted that God would take care of his family. And when he still became worried, he sought and found strength in prayer.

That was what Greven lacked, and he thought a lot about it during these final hours of his life. As a youngster he had always been indifferent and careless about faith. He was interested only in having a good time. As he grew up he became more serious, but he had never wanted anything to do with Bible reading, praying, or going to church.

Why had he joined the Resistance? Simply because he loved freedom and because he hated the Germans with their threat and tyranny. He couldn't stand the sight of them but forced himself to do business with them simply to get information that would be valuable for the Resistance.

He realized that Kooiman was different. The farmer was not motivated by hatred but by love--love for God and His service, for God's church, and therefore for his country. That had become clear to Greven.

When the final moment came, Greven could be brave, but he realized he would be poor compared to the riches Kooiman possessed.

The day passed slowly. Darkness came early in this depressing concrete bunker. High above them the small barred window allowed in only a bit of light at the best of times. By the angle of the shadows cast by the bars, the prisoners could judge roughly what time it was. This would have been supper time for most people.

Suddenly there was a noise in the corridor. The cell doors were unlocked and opened.

What could that be? More questioning? This time both men were told to get out.

Outside there were ten soldiers, all armed, waiting for the two men.

The prisoners were not handcuffed. The Germans escorted them to a large army truck, pushed them in, and then jumped in behind them.

Greven took a quick look around the truck, and he spotted what he had half expected to see—a couple of shovels lying in a corner. There was no doubt about it anymore. They would be taken out to some deserted spot, told to dig their own graves, and then shot.

Kooiman had seen the shovels also. Just for a moment, the two men looked at each other. Then the non-com in charge told them to sit down on a bench up front.

The vehicle drove off, and through the back of the truck, the two men caught glimpses of the village they were leaving behind.

Then they picked up speed and roared along a winding road flanked by trees and bushes full of new leaves.

It was a beautiful sunny spring evening. Kooiman and Greven were amazed to see so much green already. Everything testified to the coming of spring, but for them there was nothing but death ahead.

No, Kooiman checked himself, it wasn't the end. Life followed death. He would be with his Saviour, and his body would one day be resurrected in glory.

Greven's train of thought was different; he was still hoping to escape. He wasn't handcuffed, and he knew this area perfectly. Perhaps if

112

he suddenly jumped up and started flaying about with his fist, he could get away.

Common sense told him he didn't stand a chance. He would have to fight his way out between two rows of soldiers. The two men sitting in the back had their rifles ready and would open fire the minute he stood up. But despite the impossible odds, he kept hoping for an opportunity to escape.

The truck turned right, and Greven realized where they were heading. "The Baltsheide," he whispered. Other Resistance people had been executed there.

"*Nicht quatschen!*"[21] the non-com snarled. Greven fell back into silence and stared dejectedly at the marvellous sunny spring day.

There was yet another curve in the road, and suddenly the noise of the truck engine was drowned out by other sounds. The truck driver made a desperate effort to wheel his vehicle about. As he was trying to turn, the truck was hit by a hail of machine gun bullets. The driver was killed instantly, and the truck smacked into a tree and stopped dead still.

In the back, neither the prisoners nor the soldiers knew what had happened. A machine gun bullet had struck the side of the truck just above Kooiman's head, and one of the German soldiers had been wounded in the shoulder. The crash that followed the shots sent everybody tumbling across the floor.

By the time the occupants scrambled up, there were three Canadian soldiers at the back of the truck, aiming their submachine guns at the Germans.

"Hands up!" When the German non-com reached for his gun, he was sent hurtling through the truck by a burst from a Canadian submachine gun. His soldiers had already given up and quietly jumped down from the back of the truck, holding their hands high in the air.

Greven and Kooiman wisely raised their hands too. After all, their liberators couldn't tell from their faces that they were with the Resistance! But as the Germans were looking dejected, the two Dutchmen

---

[21] No talking!

were overcome with joy. The shadow of death had suddenly changed into liberty.

Their delight increased when they jumped down out of the truck. They were greeted by a man wearing a mustache and spectacles, but they had no trouble recognizing him. It was Blankers.

Since there was no time for lengthy explanations, Kooiman and Greven simply told Blankers that they had been on the way to their execution. Blankers told them that he and Cor had slipped through the German lines and joined the Canadians the day before. This very morning they had come along as guides on a mission behind enemy lines. It was a miracle of God that they had just come at the right time to save their friends from a certain death.

Cor, who was fairly skilled with the English language, spoke to the Canadians. They had no reason to distrust Kooiman and Greven! That they had had a hard time in German hands could be seen in the cuts and bruises on their faces. The Canadians treated the two men with all kinds of goodies.

The commanding officer needed information before he could decide what to do. His reconnaissance mission had been a solid success so far. They had managed to slip through German lines completely unopposed. Their encounter with the truck was the first skirmish of the day. But now they had to decide on something. Should they return to their lines before nightfall, or capture a fortified position? The latter was more appealing, of course, but it was also very risky.

The Canadian officer pulled out a technical manoeuvres map.Blankers' town was in an ideal position to become a base for further raids. Could it be taken by such a small force? Had the Germans reinforced it? And what about the population? Could they be counted on to help if needed?

After Cor translated the questions, Kooiman seemed to have second thoughts. The population could be trusted, alright. But the town had only a small squad of Resistance men, and they lacked adequate weapons. What was more, the Germans had reinforced the town because of its strategic location. There were quite a few German soldiers in town, and not far away was the main body of the Wehrmacht.

114

Greven's information was more specific. He showed the Canadians all the German defensive positions as well as the locations of their heavy guns.

The Canadian officer was astonished by Greven's detailed knowledge. Now that he knew exactly where the Germans were, he was tempted to take the town because it would enable him to harass the enemy from the rear.

But was it right to ask this of his men, especially with a Wehrmacht division only about twenty kilometres away? After a few minutes of deliberation, he shook his head; the risks were just too great. They had better go back.

The four Dutch civilians were keenly disappointed, especially Blankers. All day long he had been hoping and dreaming that he would be able to come back to town and to his wife and children as one of the town's liberators.

Greven spoke up again. He grinned broadly and said, "We can take the town with very little bloodshed. I know a back door that's not locked." He leaned over the map and pointed.

"This is a minor road into town, and the Germans won't be expecting our entry there. There's a bridge here with a single sentry. The bridge has been rigged to blow up, but what the Germans don't know is that I removed the explosives one night. Once we're across the bridge we can storm right into the middle of town."

Again Cor translated, and immediately the Canadian commanding officer saw the challenge. He discussed it with his men, and now they wanted to take the risk.

The officer gave his orders. Time was important now because they needed the element of surprise. In all probability, nobody back in town knew anything about the capture of the German truck. The gunfire couldn't possibly have been heard so far away.

Greven joined the commanding officer in his armoured car. Cor, Blankers, and Kooiman, armed with confiscated German rifles and assisted by a couple of Canadian soldiers, would guard the German prisoners inside the German army truck, which followed at the rear of the small column.

Greven directed them down the quiet country road until they came to the brick street that led to the bridge. They were hidden by trees until the last three hundred metres. There the road ran between open fields. Once they got there they increased their speed.

Greven felt almost sick with tension as they approached the bridge. If the Germans had detected his sabotage and had replaced his block of wood with more dynamite, this manoeuvre would end in disaster. He felt responsible for his friends' lives.

Two hundred metres to go. Two German soldiers came charging out of the bridge station. One of them ran to a machine gun emplacement and opened fire immediately. The other quickly sized up the situation and ducked back into the building to detonate the charge under the bridge.

A hail of machine gun bullets bounced harmlessly off the armoured car. The driver tried to jam the accelerator down even farther. Now the first armoured car clattered onto the bridge. If the bridge was going to blow at all, this was the time.

The sentry had already pushed down the button. He waited anxiously for two or three seconds, keeping his arm in front of his face to protect it from flying glass.

Nothing happened. Three times he desperately slammed down the button, but nothing happened.

Greven's relief was no less than the German's dismay.

The machine gunner threw up his hands to surrender. Because the Canadian commanding officer had given strict orders not to fire unless necessary, the man was allowed to live.

A minute later both Germans had been disarmed and loaded into the back of the truck with the other prisoners. Then on they went down the dike at top speed until they reached the outskirts of town. The villagers' mouths dropped open when they saw the heavily armoured cars roar past. What could be going on?

The Germans were no less astonished. The Ortskommandant had just been notified about the fighting at the bridge. He had sent a couple of men to see what was going on. After all, he reasoned, the Canadians weren't supposed to be anywhere around here yet. But reality hit him painfully when he saw a unit of armoured cars storming into town.

German machine guns opened fire fast. A bazooka destroyed one of the armoured cars. The rest of the armoured cars opened up with cannon fire, however, and soon the two mansions that housed the German garrison had been reduced to rubble.

Most of the Germans surrendered almost immediately, but there was a small platoon in the steeple of the municipal hall that refused to give up. The steeple's brick walls were about half a metre thick. Cannons could destroy the walls eventually, but that was probably not the best solution.

The Canadian commanding officer asked for volunteers to storm the building. Ten Canadians and four Dutch civilians prepared for the attack.

They were quickly given concise instructions. A couple of cannons opened fire on the steel-plated oak doors of the building and opened the way. A machine gunner at the base of the tower fired through the opening. Then the fourteen volunteers charged in.

Cor had been given a Dutch flag for the top of the steeple. He was right up there with the rest of them, the flag in his left hand and a pistol in his right.

Furious hand-to-hand combat raged in the tower. But in less than five minutes, it was all over. The few remaining Germans were taken prisoner. The town had been conquered. The Germans who were still hiding in fortified positions outside town wouldn't be able to do anything now that their supplies had been cut off.

Cor lay on the floor of the church. He had been struck in the chest, and his blood stained the flag. Blankers bent over him with tears in his eyes.

The Canadians were tending to their own wounded. Aided by Kooiman and Greven, Blankers carried Cor outside. He put him down on a blanket at the base of the tower. They didn't dare move him any farther because they didn't know how seriously he was wounded.

Blankers unbuttoned Cor's jacket and tried to stop the bleeding with his handkerchief, but something told him that this time Cor wouldn't recover.

The last rays of the sun touched Cor's face. He had slipped into semiconsciousness, but now he opened his eyes briefly. Blankers bent down to hear what he was trying to say.

Cor whispered, "I'm going to die, but it's okay. I'm very thankful for your friendship, Gerard, and especially . . . about what you . . . told me last night . . . I . . . I needed that."

He fell silent. Then he smiled again, more broadly. With his last energy he sighed, "I was around for the liberation after all. God is good."

He lapsed into unconsciousness again. His life was ebbing away. Only minutes later with a slight tremor, he was gone.

"It's all over," Greven said softly. Blankers wept. He had liked Cor very much.

The market square was crowded with people who were singing and dancing. An elderly gentleman elbowed his way roughly through the crowd. It was Doctor Jager.

He approached the tower and bent down over Cor's body, examining it carefully.

After several seconds he stood up. "He's gone, poor man."

Blankers spread the red, white, and blue flag over Cor's body in farewell to his friend.

By now the whole town was buzzing with activity. Men wearing orange armbands appeared and volunteered to help drive the last of the Germans from their defenses outside the town. Others began to round up members of the N.S.B. and their associates. Amid loud jeering and laughing, the mayor, Hanekroot, and Jonas Krom were taken away before they could escape.

Just then, Blankers was grabbed from behind. He wheeled around to see the joyful weeping faces of his wife and daughter Treesa. They grabbed him and held him as if they would never let go. The joy of this reunion helped to soften some of his grief for his dead friend.

Presently three boys came charging across the square at top speed.

"Dad!" Kris and Jan shouted, the first one charging at Kooiman, the second at Blankers. It was a precious moment for all of them, including Jaap, who had begun to look upon the Kooimans as his parents.

Kooiman left soon with his two boys, looking for his wife.

A small army of townspeople came toward Gerrit Greven. They had learned from the Canadians that the dealer had been their guide and that he had earlier dared to remove German explosives from the bridge. A couple of members of the Resistance had chimed in to tell about the important role Greven had played for all the past years.

Needless to say, the townspeople were deeply grateful. While they had hated the man with a passion he had been risking his life for his country! They felt they had a lot to set straight.

"Long live Gerrit Greven!" they shouted in chorus. And though the dealer struggled to get away, he was quickly hoisted up on some shoulders and triumphantly paraded through the town.

Blankers and his wife, flanked by Jan and Treesa, started for home. He had told them about Cor and his sacrifice. One last time he glanced at the face of the man who had become such a good friend and had sacrificed his life for his dear country. Then they hurried away to the younger children who were waiting at home.

The setting sun had already dropped behind the rooftops, and most of the street was shadowed. Only the steeple was still shining in the late sunlight. Someone had hung an enormous flag on top with a long orange pennant above it. The cheerful red, white, and blue snapped smartly in the brisk evening breeze, signalling an end to five years of oppression and promising a better tomorrow.

END OF BOOK